AFTER ONE
FORBIDDEN
NIGHT...

BY
AMBER McKENZIE

MILLS & BOON

Published in Great Britain 2014
by Mills & Boon, an imprint of Harlequin (UK) Limited,
Eton House, 18-24 Paradise Road, Richmond, Surrey, TW9 1SR

© 2014 Amber Whitford-McKenzie

ISBN: 978-0-263-90789-6

Harlequin (UK) Limited's policy is to use papers that are natural,
renewable and recyclable products and made from wood grown in
sustainable forests. The logging and manufacturing processes conform
to the legal environmental regulations of the country of origin.

Printed and bound in Spain
by Blackprint CPI, Barcelona

Amber McKenzie's love of romance and all the drama a good romance entails began in her teenage years. After a lengthy university career, multiple degrees and one formal English class, she found herself happily employed as a physician and happily married to her medical school sweetheart.

She rekindled her passion for romance during her residency and began thinking of the perfect story. She quickly decided that the only thing sexier than a man in scrubs was a woman in scrubs. After finishing training and starting her practice she started writing her first novel. Harlequin's *So You Think You Can Write* contest came at a perfect time, and after a few good edits from her wildlife biologist childhood best friend the manuscript was submitted. The rest is history!

Amber currently lives in Canada with her husband. She does her best to juggle her full-time medical practice with her love of writing and reading and other pursuits—from long-distance running to domestic goddess activities like cooking and quilting. Multitasking has become an art form and a way of life.

A recent title by Amber McKenzie:

RESISTING HER EX'S TOUCH

Dedication

To my Maebyn, who was a dream in my heart
when this book began and a reality in my arms
when it finished. Thank you for teaching me the joys
and discomforts of pregnancy and motherhood.
It's been an incredible adventure that is only beginning.

PROLOGUE

"DR. DARCY TO Trauma One. Dr. Darcy to Trauma One."

As always her heart began to pound and her attention became focused only on the task ahead of her. Traumas were the scariest and most rewarding part of emergency medicine. By moving and thinking quickly you could become the difference between life and death, and chief emergency resident Chloe Darcy was always half terrified and half exhilarated by the challenge.

She ran to the trauma bay and arrived as the paramedics were wheeling a patient in on a gurney. She took in the unconscious pale thin girl as the paramedics gave their report.

"Twenty-two-year-old female found unconscious by her roommate with bilateral lacerations to the wrists. Estimated blood loss at the scene was minimum one and a half liters. No signs of other trauma or drugs at the scene. She left a note. Apparently heartbroken over a recent breakup. Valentine's is the worst reminder."

Foolish girl, Chloe thought to herself. *What love or man could possibly be worth killing yourself for?*

"What has she been given for resuscitation so far?" Chloe asked, focusing on the medical care of the young woman.

"Two liters of intravenous crystalloid and five hundred

milliliters of colloid expander. Her pressure has improved marginally and the pressure dressings have stemmed some of the loss."

"Thanks, we'll take it from here."

The trauma team was a well-oiled machine, with a nursing team and a respiratory therapist working with Chloe to stabilize the young woman. It took thirty minutes and a lot of blood products and fluid before her blood pressure started to improve and her pulse lowered. Chloe felt her own do the same. Once she was confident the resources were in place to deal with additional bleeding, Chloe unwrapped the first wrist pressure bandage.

The deep lacerations exposed multiple cut vessels, tendons and nerves. The girl had really meant it, and if hadn't been for her roommate she would have succeeded.

"Page whoever is on call for Vascular and tell them we need them now." Chloe didn't have time to talk on the phone. The unwrapping of the wound had led to another half-liter blood loss and she had to focus on getting her as stable as possible prior to the operating room.

As Chloe stood above the girl, holding as tightly to the pressure bandage as she could, she felt a change in the room and calm passed over her. She looked up as Dr. Tate Reed entered. As always, her heart stopped momentarily as she took him in. His tall stature and muscular frame was surprisingly well defined beneath the hospital scrubs. His most striking features, his cool mineral-green eyes, were directed right at her.

She was surprised to see him. Normally she would have gotten the general surgery resident responsible for the vascular service, not the attending vascular surgeon. She swallowed and tried to focus on her responsibility and duty to her patient.

"What do you have, Chloe?" His voice was both confident and undemanding. He walked over to stand directly beside her while she continued to hold pressure on the volatile wound.

"Twenty-two-year-old female. Attempted suicide with bilateral wrist lacerations. Total blood loss estimated at two liters. Both cuts are deep and involve all the major vessels, nerves and tendons."

She began to unwrap the wrist so he could examine the patient for himself, when his hand came down on her bare forearm.

"Don't unwrap it, I trust you," he confided.

He looked at her one more time before moving his hand and speaking to the room. "I'll book her as level E0 emergency. Please have her ready for the operating room in the next ten minutes. I'll need another five units of blood typed and crossed and sent directly to the operating room."

With a final glance in her direction he left. She stood still, focused only on holding pressure for several moments before she regained her momentum. "Type and cross for the five units. She'll need a Foley catheter to monitor urinary output and we need to notify the plastic surgeon on call that he will be needed after Dr. Reed finishes the vascular repair."

As promised, the operating room was ready for her patient within ten minutes, and only as the young woman was being wheeled into the actual operating theater did Chloe let go her hold on the injured wrist.

When she returned to the emergency department she was grateful that there were only twenty minutes left of her shift and that she wasn't obligated to start with any new patients. It hurt her to think about the girl. How bad did you have to feel before you would go to that length to escape? How much pain did you have to be in to make the idea of cutting yourself open feel better? The only comfort Chloe had was that the girl was with Tate now, and he would at least be able to make her physically better.

Chloe finished her charting and paperwork and then went upstairs to the operating room waiting area to wait for news. The only part of emergency medicine she struggled with was the lack of continuity. She would often see patients, diagnose them, arrange for their care, but rarely learned about outcomes—and it bothered her. It was like starting a book but never finishing it, and she never felt able to accept the not knowing. Some of her evaluations had cited this as a criticism. The amount of extra time and effort she spent following up on patients was not insignificant, but it was always her own time, so those who did not like it just had to deal with it—it was who she was.

It was eleven in the evening before Tate emerged into the main operating corridor. "Why am I not surprised to see you?" he commented as he came to sit on the chair next to her, pulling the scrub cap from his head and running his fingers through his short-cropped dark blond hair. There was no censure in his voice, and he looked tired but not displeased at the sight of her.

"How is she?" Chloe asked, focusing on the reason she was there—for the girl, not for Tate.

"Stable. She was well-resuscitated prior to arrival, which helped. They were all clean cuts, which made the re-anastomosis easier. Plastics is with her now. They will be there for a couple of hours, then time will tell how much function she gets back in her hands."

"Damn," she said aloud, unable to comprehend how this girl was going to cope both physically and emotionally when she awoke.

"Any idea why she did it?" Tate asked, once again demonstrating the compassion that set him apart from many of his surgical colleagues.

"Happy Valentine's Day," Chloe responded, unable to keep the sarcasm and scorn out of her voice.

"Ah," Tate replied, obviously oblivious to the holiday. "I didn't get you anything."

The comment surprised her, but when she looked back at Tate his signature sarcastic humor glinted in the smile on his face. He had a slight curl in his lip, fitting against the sharp angle of his jaw and the clean lines of his face. She couldn't help but smile back at him.

"I'd settle for a glass of wine," she responded, and smiled until the expression on his face changed.

His smile had vanished and he was staring at her, but what he was seeing or thinking she had no idea. She didn't know what to say or do to break the silence, so instead she said nothing.

"Done."

She felt her eyes widen with surprise and remained lost for words.

"But it will have to be at my place. I didn't bring street clothes to change into and I'd rather not go out in scrubs."

She took in everything about him. He was certain in his offer, and for that reason alone she agreed.

She watched as he opened the solid metal door to his penthouse loft. She had never been inside Tate's loft before, but wasn't surprised that the interior matched the man. There was a wall of floor-to-ceiling glass that overlooked the Charles River. In true loft style there were no partitions, with the living room flowing into the dining room and kitchen. She turned and felt her heart race and warmth pass through her when she spotted the bedroom area, which featured a king-size bed raised up on a two-step platform with an exposed stone wall as the background.

There was nothing cold about the industrial style—

nothing cold at all as she admired the double-sided glass fireplace that centered the room.

Tate walked past her, his arm brushing against hers. She felt a tremor of heat pass through her and touched the area, expecting her arm to be warm. He made his way to the fridge and opened a bottle of white wine, pouring her a single glass and grabbing a beer for himself. He'd remembered what she liked and she felt the same warmth his touch had inspired run through her again.

"Make yourself at home. I'll be right back."

He gestured to the slate-gray couch that paralleled the fireplace and she did as she was told. He emerged from the closed bathroom moments later, dressed in jeans and a long-sleeved red shirt that clung to his skin, defining the muscles beneath. His feet were bare, and if she had ever doubted the magnitude of his sexuality she didn't now.

She looked at her reflection in the glass of the fireplace and for the first time in years felt dull in comparison. Her barely controllable red hair, long legs and unconcealed curves and rich emerald-green eyes typically made her stand out—but not next to Tate.

He joined her on the couch and she took a sip of the cool dry wine to calm herself. "So why is it that the most beautiful and sought-after woman in the hospital is alone on Valentine's Day?"

Beautiful? Did he really think she was the most beautiful woman in the hospital? Sought-after? Did that mean he believed the rumors that she'd used her beauty to get ahead of her peers? Looking into the cool green of his eyes, she saw no malice in the comment but she wasn't prepared to answer truthfully none the less. She was alone on Valentine's Day because the only man she was attracted to and had had feelings for in the past three years was sitting beside her and up until a few months ago had been taken by her best friend.

"I could ask you the same thing," she replied, trying to keep their conversation light and her feelings hidden. Tate was off-limits. He had been as Kate's boyfriend and he still was as Kate's ex.

"You think I'm beautiful?" He smiled, a teasing glint in his eye.

"I think you're sought-after," she answered, envisioning the trail of nurses who seemed to materialize around him.

"Not by everyone." His tone had changed and his eyes had darkened almost imperceptibly. She knew he was thinking of her best friend Kate, his ex-girlfriend—the one that had got away.

Regret and frustration coursed through her. She hadn't meant to bring up Kate, but truthfully she was always there between them. She had met Tate when he and Kate had started dating, and had been horrified when she'd realized her feelings for him went beyond friendship. It had been like a cruel torture. The closer he had become with Kate, the more she had gotten to know him, the more her feelings had grown, and the more unattainable he had become.

Kate and Tate's breakup had been bittersweet. She no longer had to conceal her feelings but she had also lost her connection to the man she was falling for.

Chloe felt as if she was burning up and moved to take off the black sweater wrap that she had layered over a long-bodied tank top. The long-sleeved tailed garment had been wrapped around her tightly against the winter cold and she felt flustered in her attempt to disentangle herself from it. Strong hands covered hers, stilling her actions, before he moved on to untying the knot in the tails, his hands sure and steady as he opened the garment and slipped it from her shoulders. In doing so the tips of his fingers brushed against her bare skin, the action causing shockwaves to course down her body. She shuddered in response.

"I thought you were too warm—are you cold?" Tate asked.

No trace of his self-defeat was left, and Chloe felt as if she had one hundred percent of his attention.

"No."

He rested his hands back on her bare arms, as if to check her temperature himself, and once again she trembled in response.

"You did it again." He was analyzing her, trying to make sense of her reactions.

"I know." What else could she say? She might not be able to control her body's reactions to him, but at least she could control her words.

His hands moved up her body, his fingers pressing into the muscles of her neck while his thumbs brushed against her cheeks. Cool mineral-green eyes stared at her hard before his lips parted. "Why are you here, Chloe?"

She closed her eyes and savored the feeling, waiting for their connection to break. She didn't want to answer the question, but she had no choice.

"Because you asked me." She opened her eyes to find Tate's entire attention focused on her, and she felt naked underneath his intense gaze. The only part of her body he touched was her neck and her face, but it was as though she could feel him all over, with every part of her body yearning to be touched by him.

"Why?" he asked, not pulling her toward him but not releasing her from his hold.

There were so many reasons that she couldn't describe them, and she wasn't sure he would understand.

She wet her lips that suddenly seemed as dry as the desert and dared to match his gaze. "Does it matter?"

The look in his eyes changed slightly, and there was a barely perceptible turn of his head. "Not tonight."

Her lips parted in response, but before the words came out his mouth came down on hers. His lips were hard against hers and he used them to tug and draw her lower lip to him. As she moaned he moved inside her, his tongue exploring and tasting what she offered. Never had she been kissed like this, and she felt helpless to hold back—not that she wanted to.

She turned her body towards him and wrapped her arms around him, her fingers moving through his hair and pressing into his scalp. He kissed her harder, deeper, his fingers tangling in *her* hair, while his other hand trailed the length of her back. She arched in response to his touch, pressing herself against him and increasing their contact.

As suddenly as the kiss had started Tate broke away from her and stood from the couch. The hand he extended toward her quickly pacified her sense of loss. Without words, she placed her hand in his and let him pull her from the couch. She trailed him as he led her to the bedroom platform. At the edge of the bed she watched him pull off the shirt that she'd thought left little to the imagination—until she saw him in the flesh. Every muscle was perfect and defined. She reached out and let her fingers softly move over the strong breadth of his shoulders, his chest, and then along his washboard abdomen until they ended at the top of his belt and jeans.

He started in the same place, his hands moving around her waist as his fingers grabbed enough fabric to pull the tank top from her body. She had never felt self-conscious about her body, but at that moment she felt very aware of the state of her own arousal. Tate's hand encircled her waist again, but this time over the bare skin he had exposed. She shuddered at the heat she felt coming from his touch and felt him pull her to him in response.

"Definitely not cold," she heard him whisper as his warm breath surged against her neck. His lips followed as he found her weakness, each kiss and taste stoking the fires within her. She dug her fingers into his sides and pulled him back to her and was rewarded by the hard ridge that pressed into her.

He released his hold on her as he stepped back, just far enough to remove his jeans. He held her eyes as he did the same with hers, until she was standing before him in her blue lace bra and underwear. He didn't close the distance between them and she watched his eyes trail up and down her body. It was excruciating anticipation, and she didn't know how to express what she wanted, so she echoed his earlier action and held out her hand.

He didn't take it. Instead her palm made contact with his bare chest as he reached behind her and unfastened her strapless bra. Her swollen breasts spilled out as the garment fell to the floor. She felt his fingertips brush against the sides of her breasts, then her waist, until they reached her hips and the small strings of her underwear before they too were tugged from her body. He didn't leave her naked alone, stripping himself of his last remaining article of clothing with no modesty until he stood equally naked before her.

She gasped as he lifted her up and toward him. She held on tightly, wrapping her legs around him as he held her effortlessly. She felt cool sheets touch her back as she felt the pressure and heat of Tate come down on top of her. His mouth returned to hers with the increased passion that being completely skin to skin ignited. His hand moved, sweeping the side of her breast before he finally cupped her in his hands. She moaned at the experience and her reaction was met by his lips, which closed over the opposite nipple.

She spread her legs wide beneath him—a silent plea for what she really wanted.

She watched as he reached over to the nightstand and withdrew a small foil packet. She thought she could see his hands shaking as he unrolled the condom down his impressive length. She reached out to steady his hands and in response to her gentle touch he entwined her fingers in his, moving her hand and arm over her head, pressing her into the pillow above.

He once again settled between her legs and in one precision movement filled her. The spasm of her muscles around him echoed in the grip he reinforced on her hand.

She cried out with a pleasure she had never experienced before. She wasn't a virgin, but nothing had ever felt like this before. She wrapped her legs around him, anchoring him to her as he moved within her, pushing her further and further into ecstasy with each thrust. She didn't get a break as each movement in and out of her triggered every nerve in her body to fire, until she felt she was on the verge of shattering from within. Without warning she was past the point of no return and she cried out, clutching him to her as her muscles contracted reflexively around him. One more stroke and Tate was with her, his own convulsions joining hers.

He collapsed against her and she could feel the dampness of his skin and the warmth of his breath against her neck. She couldn't resist the feel of him, satiated and relaxed against her, and gently ran her fingertips of her free hand up and down his back. It was an act of intimacy beyond the passion they had just shared.

She lost track of time, savoring the feeling of closeness, of Tate inside her, until he lifted himself away. He was staring down at her, levered above her, still deep inside her. He was looking at her for answers, for an explanation of how they'd got to where they were and what to do next. She had none.

His hand brushed her hair away from her face. "I can't talk about this right now," he said, and she heard enough regret to break her heart.

"Okay," she replied, lost for any other words. He withdrew from her body and left to go to the only closed room in the loft—the bathroom.

She sat upright and covered herself with one of the oversized pillows. She wanted to move—needed to move, needed to gather her clothes and what was left of her heart and dignity and get the hell out of there. But she couldn't move. Every muscle in her body was paralyzed by the surrealism of what had just happened. *Tate—she'd had sex with Tate*. But it hadn't just been sex. It had been the most cataclysmic physical and emotional experience of her life and in that moment she realized she loved him. And he regretted it. Did she? She had vowed never to act on her feelings, but now that she had how could she dream of taking it back?

The sound of the door opening brought her attention back to reality. Tate strode naked to the platform, with no embarrassment or attempt to hide his nudity. He was spectacular. She had never appreciated the draw of the naked male form until now. She was sure in the knowledge that the sight of him and the memory of how he'd felt inside her would be forever burned into her body, mind and soul.

He turned down the covers on his side of the bed and gestured for her to get in. It was an offer she shouldn't accept, but it was too hard to say no. As she crawled beneath the sheets he walked to the other side of the bed and did the same. He turned off the lights from a master panel on the nightstand, leaving only the amber glow of the fire and the reflection of the city's lights through the windows. She lay there still, not knowing what to say or do, until she felt his strong arm snake around her and pull her against him.

"Go to sleep," he whispered, his lips only inches from her ear and the length of his naked body pressed against her back and bottom.

Impossible was the last thing she thought, before she closed her eyes and her mind gave way to the complete physical and emotional exhaustion of her body.

Tate woke from a deep sleep and felt his body stir and harden. He wasn't alone—could feel himself pressing against soft skin and tight curves. He opened his eyes to the early-morning light and saw it: red. Red hair covered the pillow that lay beside him. Red hair that was unmistakable.

Chloe. As he acknowledged her identity in his head a replay of last night's events rolled through his mind. He could see her tremble with his touch, her nipples pressing against the thin fabric of her tank top, the way she'd let him undress her and then reached out for him. And there was the way she'd felt, tight and uncontrolled beneath him so that he had barely managed to hold on for her release.

It was painful to think about it as he felt himself engorge further, pressing deeper into her tight, rounded bottom. He wanted to kiss her neck, caress her breast and slip back inside her—in part for release, and in part to prove to himself that they hadn't been as explosive together as he remembered. But the cold light of day streaming in from the floor-to-ceiling windows stopped him.

How had he let this happen—and why? He hadn't just taken any ordinary woman to bed, he had taken Chloe. Chloe—the beautiful, smart, no-nonsense, caring woman he had known for years. It wasn't as if he had just realized Chloe's beauty. He had always felt an attraction to her. But by the time they had met he had already started pursuing Kate, and he'd classified his feelings for Chloe as those of a normal red-blooded male. What had happened last night? Damned if he knew. All he knew was that the attraction he had suppressed for years had boiled over—with considerable consequences.

He ran his fingers through the tumble of red hair adorning his pillow. This was going to end badly. He wasn't naïve about the nature of the medical profession. Women still had to work harder to prove their equality, especially in fields dominated by men. Women like Chloe—though he couldn't think of *any* woman like Chloe—had it the hardest. Looking at her, no one would imagine that she could be as smart and gifted as she was beautiful. Worse, few believed that her success was due to hard work alone.

He had heard the rumors about her and resented them. Unfortunately coming to her defense would only fuel the fire. Personally, Tate could care less what people thought or said about his personal life. He made his own decisions—for himself and no one else. But as a woman and as a resident Chloe didn't have that luxury.

The rumors would be vicious. The effect on her career would be unpredictable. And for what? What did he have to offer her? He had tried to settle down for a life of commitment and had it thrown back in his face. He wasn't prepared to go down *that* road again, but he also wasn't prepared to hurt Chloe just to satisfy a need in him he hadn't known existed until last night. He had crossed a line last night that he'd had no business crossing and hated himself for it.

He needed to end this before it started—or went any further.

* * *

Chloe stirred, her eyes opening to unfamiliar surroundings as she took in the flood of natural light and the expanse of the room around her. She blinked and the scenery remained unchanged. She looked down, acknowledging her nudity before confirming to herself that last night had not been a dream. She was in Tate's loft and they had made love.

Slowly she turned towards the other side of the bed—only to find disappointment at its emptiness. The feeling did not last long as her eyes caught sight of him sitting across the room in the kitchen, staring back at her. He appeared to have showered and was already fully dressed in black pants and a crisp navy blue button-down shirt with a pewter tie at the collar. An uneasy feeling came over her.

"Good morning." She waded into conversation cautiously.

"Last night was a mistake."

His words broke through her and her perfect dream instantaneously changed into a nightmare. He remained across the room, still making no effort to close the distance between them.

"I think it would be best if we forget it ever happened and moved on with our separate lives. Take your time this morning. I have to go to work, but the door will lock behind you."

She didn't have time to argue with him. She didn't even have time to respond. She just watched dumbstruck as Tate walked out, pulling the door shut behind him and signaling the end to their conversation. How could he just walk away? Easily, she thought. He didn't have feelings for her. A physical attraction, yes, but not the same depth of emotion she felt for him or he had felt for Kate.

She remembered him after their breakup—how

angry he had been, how devastated. She was a simple
night's mistake compared to Kate, whose loss had almost
destroyed him.

CHAPTER ONE

Six weeks later...

CHLOE STOOD FROM her chair and felt a familiar wave of nausea and dizziness encompass her. She steadied herself before considering moving again. If she had thought things couldn't get worse, she had been wrong. Her relationship with Tate remained unchanged. She had made attempts to talk to him but it was clear he was avoiding her. The hope that every day she would feel better, less rejected, was long since gone and every day she felt worse.

She needed to finish with her last patient and go home. The symptoms which she had originally attributed to heartbreak had become unremitting, and it was getting harder and harder to function. Ironically, the last patient of the evening emergency shift was feeling the same. An "LOL" in distress: a "little old lady" presenting with feelings of weakness and dizziness.

These patients were always complex, taking a lot of time and attention to detail in order to rule out conditions that could cause the patient serious harm, and most commonly nothing was found. In this case Chloe had managed to work out a cause and had reduced her blood pressure medications. If only her own case was that simple.

"Are you okay?"

A voice cut through her thoughts. She turned too quickly and immediately regretted the action, feeling her heart beat overtime to maintain her balance and remain standing on her feet.

Her attending physician, Dr. Ryan Callum, was staring at her intently and Chloe was grateful that it was him. He was seven years older than her and had completed a decorated military career as a trauma specialist before starting practice at Boston General. He was very attractive, with an athletic frame, a rare combination of brown hair and blue eyes, and a collection of scars and military tattoos that completed the package and led to him being sought after by the entire nursing staff. To Chloe, he was a trusted friend and mentor.

"I'm fine."

"You're lying." He wasn't angry, but he was making it clear he did not believe her.

"Yes, but you are a good enough friend not to push the issue."

He reluctantly nodded his agreement and Chloe relaxed. She didn't have the energy to pretend right now as she rubbed her aching shoulders.

"You would tell me if you needed something, right?"

She looked at her friend and a little bit of her misery and pity lifted. She might not have love, but she had amazing friends who would do anything for her. If only she knew how she could be fixed.

"Yes, I would."

"Okay, then, go home. You look like hell."

"Thanks, I will."

Chloe discharged her patient and made her way to the women's locker room, located within the emergency department. Her head throbbed, and pushing open the door took the last effort she had inside her. Between the rows of lockers was a bench and she'd stepped toward it, planning to rest, when a sharp pain in the right lower quadrant of her abdomen overtook her. The pain was so severe that she didn't feel the impact as her body hit the floor. She tried to call for help but didn't get the words out before curtains of black entered her vision.

Someone was screaming, but it wasn't her. Everything was muted as she struggled to see and hear what was going on around her. She felt herself being picked up and carried by a pair of strong arms.

"Tate," she whimpered as the pain gripped her again.

"No, Chloe, it's Ryan."

Disappointment filled her before she lost consciousness again.

Tate scanned the operating room slate for the night's booked cases. The locked doors to the secure unit opened and a porter entered, carrying a sealed box from the blood bank. The unit clerk who had been assisting him shifted her attention from him. "Is that the blood for Theater Seven?"

"Yes, it's the second four units of packed cells and two units of fresh frozen plasma matched for a Chloe Darcy— D-A-R-C-Y. Date of birth: March twentieth, 1983. Blood bank number: 4089213."

"Perfect. You can leave it there and I'll take it back to the room."

Tate's body had frozen at the sound of her name and his eyes landed on the box, confirming everything he had heard. The box was labeled just as the porter had read— for Chloe. He replayed the exchange. This was the second four units, which meant Chloe was in serious trouble.

"I'm already changed. I'll take it in," he told the unit clerk as he picked up the box and made his way toward Theater Seven without waiting for her response. It was ironic that for the first time in the operating room he felt fear. Never had he felt that when working, but right now he was helpless. It was a novel and terrifying feeling all at once.

He fastened a mask across his face and paused at the window in the door. There were two anesthetists at the head of the bed and the patient was surrounded, but he couldn't tell by whom. On the operating room floor a collection of bloody sponges lay soaked through and counted off. He could see the suction canisters that were filled with over two liters of blood. Was it Chloe's blood? It looked like a scene from a trauma case, and he couldn't comprehend that Chloe lay in the center of it.

He walked into the room, his confusion growing as he identified members of the gynecology team as the operating surgeons. At the same time his eyes glimpsed the trademark red hair that flowed from the top of the operating table. It was definitely her.

He handed the box to the circulating nurse. "Do you need help?" He directed the question toward the team, needing to do *something*.

"You need to leave, Dr. Reed."

The voice came from the gowned surgeon in the hibiscus-blue cloth scrub hat. He narrowed his focus on her and through the confusion surrounding the case was able to identify Erin Madden, chief gynecology resident. Her voice and hat identified her without her needing to look away from the operative field. He had known Erin casually for years, and more so in the past two through her friendship with Kate and Chloe, but even so he wasn't in the mood to be told what to do. He normally encouraged resident autonomy, but not today—not when it involved Chloe.

"Dr. Thomas?" He addressed the staff surgeon whose back was to him.

"Dr. Madden is right. This is not a vascular case, Tate. We are going to have to ask you to leave."

He looked around the room once more, noticing the discomfort of the nursing and other teams. It felt like a betrayal from the people he worked with day in and day out, but on the other hand he knew enough to know that he had become a distraction—one that Chloe couldn't afford.

"Okay." And he left, going as far away from her as he could handle being, which was right outside the operating theater doors.

His mind raced with possibilities? What the hell had happened to Chloe? How did a healthy young woman end up in a critical condition without warning? And why the hell was gynecology in there?

A previously unimaginable explanation filled and settled into his mind. He watched, his eyes oscillating between the anesthesia monitors tracking Chloe's vitals and the actions of the surgical team.

"Tate." He heard Kate's familiar voice and felt a hand on his shoulder.

"I think she is stabilizing. They kicked me out of the room, so I can't tell for sure. But they have stopped calling for blood and I can see the anesthesia monitors. Her heart-rate has come down and her blood pressure is back up."

"What happened?" Kate asked.

"I don't know. They won't tell me anything. The usual patient confidentiality. I only got here about fifteen minutes ago. I was checking the operating room slate to see how many cases were lined up for tonight at the front desk when the porter from the blood bank came to drop off blood. I overheard him verifying her name and blood bank number with the unit clerk."

"Who is in with her?"

"Gynecology." His resentment was coming through clearly.

"Oh."

"Is it a hemorrhagic ovarian cyst?" Kate asked.

"I don't know, Kate. Like I said, they won't tell me anything."

She stopped asking questions and he wondered if she had come up with the same diagnosis he had. Either way he was grateful for the silence. He needed to keep his entire focus on Chloe.

Twenty minutes later Kate gently pushed Tate to the side and went through the operating room door. He watched the interaction, unable to hear the exchange between her and Erin Madden, but noting that she was getting further than he had. She pushed through the doors again, returning.

"She's okay. They won't tell me what happened, but they opened her up, stopped whatever was bleeding, and she's stabilized. She is going to go to the Intensive Care Unit overnight because of the large amount of blood products she received."

"Thank you, Kate," Tate replied, his eyes still trained on the window, not budging from his spot outside the door.

"Tate, they have asked us to leave and I think we should. She is stable and there is nothing we can do except get in the way and distract the team."

"I'm not leaving her."

"We're not leaving her, Tate. We're helping her by getting out of the way and letting them do their job. The same thing we ask other people to do for us." She grabbed his arm and pulled him a little, to ease him away from his spot. "Tate, we need to go. You know Chloe would never want us to see her like this."

His mind replayed all the ways he had seen Chloe and he knew she was right. Staying away from her had been the hardest thing he had ever done, but it was for her he'd done it. God knew that every time she had tried to talk to him there'd been nothing he wanted more than to take her in his arms and kiss her, to see if everything they had done together had been real and not just a memory that had reached fantastical proportions in his mind.

Who was he kidding? In truth he was terrified of the feelings she'd brought out in him and what it would cost him to have and then lose her.

He looked back at Kate, feeling nothing for her. How could he have been such a fool? He respected Kate, and intellectually she made perfect sense, but he had never been in love with her and she had never sparked the intensity of emotion that Chloe did in him. He had asked her to marry him because it had seemed like the next logical step, just like the series of steps he had taken in his training. He was tired of the single life, needed a wife, wanted a family and Kate met the criteria he was looking for. His use of logic had failed him for the first time in his life. Kate's rejection had angered him and wounded his pride at the time. Now he was grateful for the near miss.

"Are you in love with Matt McKayne?" he asked, without emotion.

She seemed surprised by the question, whether it was at his directness or his reference to the man he knew she was in love with, he didn't care.

"Yes. I think I always have been—even when I hated him."

"Then you should be with him. Forget everything that has gone wrong between you and be together."

"It's not that simple, Tate. I can't trust him."

"Kate, *that's* not simple," he replied, pointing toward the door. Then he took one last look through the window and walked away—from both Chloe and Kate.

His steps were slow and purposeful as he returned to the front desk and the unit clerk he had spoken to earlier. He took a deep breath, steeling himself for the response he was dreading. "Am I up next after the ruptured ectopic pregnancy?" he asked as casually as he could while his heart was racing.

He held his breath as the unit clerk double-checked the confidential surgical slate that listed patient names, procedures and diagnoses. "Yes. As soon as they are done with Dr. Darcy we will be sending for your patient, Dr. Reed."

"Thank you," he mumbled and he kept walking, not thinking about his destination but more of the confirmation he had hoped not to receive. Chloe was pregnant—or had been pregnant. Was he the father? Was he responsible for the pregnancy that had almost killed her?

The door to the operating room opened again and Ryan Callum walked through.

"Is she still in?" Ryan asked, with a coldness Tate had not expected emanating from him.

He wasn't in the mood to play games. "Yes. Do you know what happened to her?"

"Yes."

Tate waited, but no more words came from the other man and new hostility radiated from him. Ryan, who had never been confrontational, had changed from the direct, no-nonsense man he had been. The question was why? In a night with so many unanswered questions it was the last thing he needed.

"I'm asking," Tate replied, not trying to escalate the conversation, knowing he had a thin grip on his temper.

"If Chloe wanted you to know something she would have told you."

Told him what? That there was a reason Ryan Callum knew about her pregnancy and he didn't? It was a thought he couldn't stomach and he wanted it out of his mind.

"What's that supposed to mean?"

"You're the brilliant surgeon, Tate, figure it out."

He didn't want to have to think about any more than

he already was. At the moment he would much rather be the father of her life-threatening pregnancy than think there was a possibility that Ryan was.

"So I'm to blame? Is that what you think?"

"She said your name, not mine, as I carried her near lifeless body to get help. That is what I think."

The image flashed before his eyes, and judging from the scene in the operating theater Tate knew Ryan's characterization was right. Before he could respond Ryan walked past him toward the bank of theaters, which was fortunate because he had no response. Did that mean he was the father? Ryan hadn't ruled himself out, but what did it say about Chloe that she would ask for *him* as she lay dying?

CHAPTER TWO

EVERYTHING HURT. IT was her first thought as outside sounds began to intrude. She tried to move, to ease the ache, but nothing in her body responded. She took a breath and became immediately cognizant of pain and pressure in her mouth and throat. She tried to pull at it, but couldn't move her hands. When she finally moved she felt the resistance of straps on her wrists.

A monitor rang out and it calmed her as a familiar sound. She felt a hand curl around hers and tried to hold it.

"Chloe, it's Kate."

Kate. She didn't know where she was, but Kate was here. She heard her friend's voice again, but couldn't make out the words. She strained to understand, wanted to move, to breathe, but everything was so hard and met with such resistance.

She heard the alarm ring again as she struggled.

Someone with a voice she didn't recognize entered the room and she could hear Kate directing the woman before she felt a hand calmingly stroke her forehead and hair.

She only understood a few of Kate's words but it was enough. "Stay calm, okay? Intubated…Intensive Care Unit…tube out. Stay calm."

She focused all her efforts on opening the heavy lids of her eyes to see Kate as her dark hair and her face slowly came into focus. She had to work twice as hard not to give in to the temptation to close them again.

There was another voice she didn't recognize, and once again she couldn't understand everything, so instead focused on Kate.

"Chloe, you heard that? I have to go for a few minutes while they evaluate you. No room for big dumb surgeons on these occasions. I am not going to be far, though, and will be back here as soon as they let me, okay?"

She processed the information and finally, with great effort, managed to move her head in understanding. She watched Kate's eyes fill with relief and felt her friend squeeze her hand one last time before she left.

Over the next few minutes she was aware of the room filling with more and more people. She was also aware that if she wanted the tube out she was going to have to concentrate on everything she was being asked to do, even though it was a struggle. After what seemed like a lifetime she took her first breath on her own, and even the irritation in her throat couldn't dampen her relief. She felt a nurse thread the oxygen nasal prongs around her face and into her nose as air gently began to blow, and she was grateful for anything that made breathing less hard.

As fast as the room had filled it began to empty, until only one person remained. With only one person to focus on it was easier, and she recognized the face, dark tortoiseshell glasses and pulled-back blonde hair of her friend Erin Madden pulling up a chair beside the bed. Through her emerging fog she could tell Erin wasn't here as her friend. Why was gynecology involved in her care?

"Chloe, do you know where you are?"

She nodded, her mind having put together the fact that she was in the Intensive Care Unit.

"Did you know you were pregnant?" Erin asked softly.

Pregnant. No. That couldn't be right. She couldn't be

pregnant. She had only been with one man in the past two years and Tate had worn a condom. Wouldn't she have known if she was pregnant? She had been bleeding off and on for the past month, but her cycle was screwed up because of all the stress. She had been nauseated and dizzy, but that could be stress too. Wouldn't she have known if she was pregnant with Tate's baby? A warm flush passed through her as she thought about a child.

"I'm pregnant?" she managed to ask, her voice still weak.

"No, Chloe. You *were* pregnant. The pregnancy was ectopic, in your right fallopian tube. It ruptured. That is what led to your collapse. We did an emergency laparotomy and had to take out your right fallopian tube to stop the bleeding. You also were transfused with a lot of blood products, so we decided to keep you in the Intensive Care Unit. But you are okay now, Chloe. Your blood work is stable and there are no signs of anymore bleeding. You are going to be okay."

"I lost the baby." It wasn't a question for Erin, but more a confirmation to herself of everything she had just heard.

"Yes. I'm so sorry, Chloe."

Grief filled her. It was the final insult. It shouldn't hurt to lose something she had never known she had, but that didn't stop the pain. Maybe it was fitting that she felt the same way about her baby's father. She had never had him either, but that didn't make losing him any easier.

She looked around the room, surrounded by glass and curtains and monitors that would show everything about her. She didn't want to be here.

"I want to go home, Erin. I *need* to go home." She couldn't be here—not in public, not where she worked, not where Tate worked. Not knowing he was so close and wanting him to be with her at this moment so very badly and knowing he wouldn't be coming.

"Chloe, you are barely twenty-four hours post-op. You know you are in no condition to go home. You just started breathing on your own and haven't even sat up yet."

She tried to push herself up, to prove that she could do it, but her body betrayed her. Between the physical exertion the act required and the sense of dizziness that swept over her she barely lifted herself for a few seconds before collapsing.

"Chloe, please let me handle this. I am going to have you transferred to Obstetrics, where no one knows you and you can have some privacy."

She knew she didn't have a choice. She couldn't leave even if she wanted to. The obstetrics ward... Pregnant woman and babies... Could she do that? Now? On the other hand Erin was right—it was a ward where no one would know her.

"Okay," she assented, before closing her eyes, exhausted physically and emotionally. She felt Erin pull the blankets over her. "Thank you for everything," she managed, right before sleep overtook her.

Chloe stirred, the pain in her abdomen still sharp and making her restless. She felt a hand sweep her hair from her face. Kate. She had told her best friend to go home but apparently she hadn't listened.

Pain coursed through her as she tried in vain to find a comfortable position and a soft moan escaped her.

A hand fell onto her arm and she instantly knew that it was not Kate beside her. The hand was heavy and large and she recognized Tate's touch. She didn't open her eyes. She wasn't ready to face him. She heard her call bell go off and Tate asking for a nurse.

The exchange was brief, and within five minutes Chloe felt some of the pain dissipate from her body—but not her heart.

"I know you are not sleeping, Chloe."

Tate's voice broke through her thoughts. She opened her eyes to meet his. Each of them was trying to decipher the other. He looked tired, with new shadowing along his face and a redness in his eyes that served to heighten the light green irises. Despite her need for him she felt overwhelmed by his presence.

"How did you know?" she whispered.

"Because I've watched you sleep," he answered, as though the statement held no intimacy.

"No, I mean how did you know I was here?" she asked, not wanting to betray any of the information she had barely had time to digest.

"I'm on nights this week and saw you in the operating room."

She grimaced at the thought of him seeing her exposed—not one she enjoyed.

"Is the morphine not enough? Do you need something else?" he asked, misreading her cue.

"No, I'm fine." A complete overstatement, but she felt vulnerable and not ready for this conversation.

"You scared me."

The honesty in his face and his statement humbled her.

"I'm sorry."

"Is there a reason you didn't tell me?" His voice had quietened.

"What do you mean?" He was searching for an answer but she didn't understand the question.

Tate stared at her as though he could learn the answer if he just looked hard enough. She looked back at him, equally searching for an answer. "Was there a reason you didn't tell me about the pregnancy?"

He knew. She didn't know how, but he did. He probably had known before she did. Just one more insult in what was already an untenable situation. He was asking her if he was the father of her baby. What must he think of her if he thought there might be more than one possibility?

She blinked hard, trying to calm herself against the ugliness she felt inside. When she opened her eyes he was still staring at her, waiting.

"Does it matter, Tate?" The hurt in her voice was apparent even to her own ears.

"Yes, it matters."

"Why?" she demanded.

"It just does, Chloe."

"Because if you were the father then, what? You would take pity on me? Feel guilty? But if you weren't then everything people say about me must be right and you can walk away and count your blessings for your near miss? I'm sorry, Tate, but neither of those options works for me. I think you should go."

"We're not done, Chloe."

She wanted to cry and tried hard to keep in her tears. She took a deep breath to steady herself. "Be honest with yourself, Tate. We never started. I need you to go."

"What if I want to stay, Chloe?"

"Then you should have stayed six weeks ago. Or at least listened to me when I tried to talk to you afterward. But you wanted nothing to do with me then, and you don't get to change your mind now. I want you to leave." She could hear the pleading in her voice but she didn't care. She couldn't do this—not now, when she had already depleted every physical and emotional resource she had.

"But the baby...?" His voice was hushed but still she heard the small crack that betrayed him.

"There is no baby," she told them both, and the words hurt as much as anything she had felt. Tate blurred before her eyes and she couldn't read him as tears formed. She watched him get up and walk away from her and felt both relieved and wounded by his departure.

She heard the curtains close and the sliding door of her intensive care room slide shut and she closed her eyes, willing the tears to stop. She couldn't do this—not here.

She barely had time to process the sound of the guard rail going down, or the weight on her bed, before she felt herself being picked up as strongly, and yet as gently as possible, and held tightly within a strong embrace. She felt pain tear through her abdomen, but it was nothing compared to what was going on in her heart. She shouldn't do this—she shouldn't feel better in Tate's arms. But she did.

Her complete loss of control over her life overwhelmed her and she gave in to the urge she had been fighting since she woke up. For some reason she knew she didn't have to be brave right now—she didn't need to put on the funny, reassuring front she had for Kate. Right now she could just *hurt* and it didn't matter. She had nothing to lose with Tate; she had lost everything already.

She felt his grip tighten as the sobs began to rack through her body, each movement both bringing and taking away the pain. He brought his chin down to rest on her head while his hand stroked up and down her back.

"I didn't know about the baby," she confessed into his already soaked scrub top.

"It'll be okay, Chloe. *You* are okay," he murmured in reassurance.

"It's not okay. How could I not have known about my own child?"

"It wouldn't have made a difference."

No, it wouldn't have. A child between them wouldn't have changed Tate's mind or his feelings toward her. "I didn't deserve a baby."

"You didn't deserve any of *this*."

"Didn't I?" She had done the unthinkable. She had fallen in love and slept with her best friend's ex, who the morning after had found her lacking. The only reason Tate was here now was because he felt sorry for her, but to be honest not more sorry than she felt for herself.

He pulled her gently away from his shoulder, reaching up to cradle her face in his hands. "No, Chloe, you didn't."

She wished she could believe him. She had never put much stock in karma before—you couldn't when you spent your life treating people you were sure didn't deserve what was happening to them. But now she wasn't sure.

She felt fresh tears forming in her eyes at the pain of her thoughts and from staring into Tate's eyes too much. He really looked as if he cared for her. If only that was the case.

She felt his lips press against the dampness of her cheek before she was once again tucked into his arms and held tightly. She didn't know how long they stayed like that. She didn't even remember him leaving. But when she woke he was gone.

Post-operative day two was excruciating. Everything felt like a struggle. First thing in the morning a nurse had come to help her "dangle', which had basically turned into a torture exercise of being forced to sit upright with her legs dangling off the bed, maintaining her balance. She'd lasted for less than five minutes and then slept for the next three hours to recover. When she woke Kate was there, propped in a bedside chair reading a heavy hardcover text that almost completely covered her. She was comforted by her friend's presence.

"Hey," Chloe greeted her, watching as Kate's focus shifted and she herself was assessed by the good surgeon.

"You look better," Kate said reassuringly.

"That's not saying much," she replied, still having to work to keep her eyes open.

"Do you want to tell me what happened?" Kate asked tentatively.

She hadn't thought about much in the last twenty-four hours, but what she *had* thought about, other than Tate and the loss of their baby, was what was she going to tell Kate?

Kate—her best friend, the person she had been closest with during the past decade. She couldn't lie, but how much of the truth was too much? Especially when the explanation for how she had gotten to this day was unexplainable even to herself.

"I had an ectopic pregnancy that ruptured." Nothing had prepared her for what she saw in Kate's face. She wasn't even sure she had been that surprised.

"I didn't realize you were in a relationship," was all Kate managed after minutes of silence.

Beyond the words she could see the hurt in her friend's eyes. The thought that Chloe had been keeping something from her was painful for Kate.

"I'm not, Kate." Truer words were never spoken.

"Oh."

She knew that Kate was not going to ask her more, but felt she owed her friend more of an explanation. "I slept with someone a few weeks ago. It was a mistake. It didn't work out."

Kate didn't respond immediately. She seemed to be processing the information until her look of surprise was replaced by one of understanding. "I'm sorry."

"So am I." And she was. A lifetime spent thinking about the man you loved who'd got away would have been better than the crash-and-burn drama that had unfolded with Tate.

"Is there anything I can do?"

"I don't suppose I can convince you to help bust me out of here?" she asked faint-heartedly, realizing that she likely couldn't even make it as far as the elevator right now.

"No, sorry. No chance of that happening. Try again."

"I would love my own clothes and stuff to take a shower."

"That I *can* do. So you'll be wanting your make-up and finest lingerie, then?"

Kate winked at her and Chloe was grateful for the lightening of their conversation.

"Definitely. Goes great with these disposable mesh underwear I am ashamed to admit are surprisingly comfortable."

"Is it hard being a patient?"

"Yes, but I haven't figured out what is worse: feeling helpless or being a patient where I work."

It was the truth. She was so used to *doing*, to being active, multi-tasking, and now she couldn't perform the simplest of tasks for herself and was dependent on people she was used to impressing with her abilities. It was hard to be this vulnerable.

"It is a big change, but the first couple of days are the worst. By tomorrow you'll be moving around a bit more and you will be home in a few days."

"Not soon enough." She waited for a while, trying to decide if she really wanted to know the answer to her next question. "Does everyone know?"

"No. The story around the emergency department and amongst some of the other services is that you had a hemorrhagic ovarian cyst. I think the residents in your program are planning on sending flowers. All your shifts have been covered for the next eight weeks so that you don't have to work before the board exam."

"Eight weeks seems like such a short and a long time all at once."

"It's not too long, Chloe. You need to focus on yourself

for once. If you had a patient who had just gone through the same experience you would counsel her the exact same way."

"I agree completely."

A new voice came from behind the curtain before it was opened to reveal Ryan Callum.

"Hi," Chloe greeted him, embarrassed again at her lack of knowledge about that night, but knowing Ryan had to have been there.

Kate rose and stared at Ryan, then at her. "I'll leave you two alone. I'll be back later this afternoon with your stuff." Kate gave her one final look and then left, pulling the curtain and the door shut behind her.

"I didn't mean to interrupt," Ryan responded, taking Kate's now vacated chair.

"You're not."

"How are you feeling?"

She could see the clinician in him assessing her and did her best to reassure him.

"I'm okay, and Kate assures me that every day is going to be a little better." She was counting on that in more ways than one. "Did you take care of me the other night?"

"Yes. I don't think I've ever been more scared."

"I'm sorry."

"Don't be. I wanted to stop by and make sure you were okay. I also wanted to make sure you knew that no one in the department other than me saw the results of your beta-HCG that night."

She felt a flush of embarrassment pass through her, but also a sense of relief at what Ryan was telling her. No one else had seen the positive pregnancy test, which explained why they all believed she had had a ruptured cyst. Having managed to maintain her privacy was a small relief.

"Thank you," she said gratefully.

"Don't thank me. I don't want anything standing between you and your future staff position here at Boston General—which, by the way, will be waiting for you whenever you are ready."

"Thank you," she said again, this time struggling to keep tears from her eyes.

"You're worth it, Chloe. Please remember that."

She could tell he was holding something back, which was far from normal. "Why do I feel like there is something you are not saying?"

"Because there is. But I don't think this is the time or any of my business."

"Since when did you hold back your praise or your criticism, Ryan?" she goaded him, not wanting anything to change in her life more than it already had.

"Tate Reed."

Her heart stopped and she briefly looked around to ensure Tate, or anyone else for that matter, had not come into her room. What else did Ryan know? What else had happened that night?

"What about Tate?"

"I want you to be careful, Chloe."

"It's a little too late for that, don't you think?" she responded, understanding that somehow Ryan knew about her involvement with Tate.

"Just be careful. I don't know Tate well, but I know his type. And if the hospital administration was ever forced to choose between their prized vascular surgeon and you, you wouldn't win."

"Tate would never..." she started, and then stopped herself. She didn't know what Tate would or wouldn't do. "Thank you, Ryan—for everything."

CHAPTER THREE

POST-OPERATIVE DAY THREE was better. She could move around her room and was able, with some assistance, to take a shower, which felt better than any pain medication she had received. Her nausea was still there, but less than what it had been, and she imagined it would be a while before all the hormones of pregnancy were cleared from her system. She used similar reasoning to explain her new-found propensity toward tears. She cried when she was frustrated, she cried when she thought about what she had lost, she even cried when the nurses were kind to her.

Kate had brought her things and she struggled to keep her eyes open as she read one of her textbooks: another attempt at distraction. A new knock at the door signaled the end of her struggle. Kate peered around the privacy curtain that separated the door from her bed, the smile on her face the first thing visible. Chloe automatically smiled back.

"I have news," Kate announced before she could even cross the room.

Chloe could tell she was barely containing herself and felt her own excitement build. She pushed herself up in bed, happy to have made the effort to put on her own clothes, even it was only her favorite yoga pants and a fitted gray sweater.

Kate pulled up the visitor's chair right beside her. "Matt has asked me to marry him and I've accepted."

"Oh, my God," Chloe gasped. One look at Kate was all it took for her tears to return. Never had she seen her so joyous. She reached up and Kate met her halfway.

"He loves me—he always has," Kate explained.

Chloe simply hugged her harder. Of course Matt loved Kate. She was perfect. She squeezed her eyes shut, trying to block out a burgeoning feeling of jealousy at all Kate had. She needed to stop this. She was lucky to be alive and she had friends she loved who loved her. She just didn't have the man she was in love with.

They broke apart and she was once again rewarded with the look of pure happiness on Kate's face.

"I wanted you to be the first to know."

"I'm so happy for you. And for Matt."

"So you'll be my maid of honor?"

"Nothing would make me happier than to stand beside you on your wedding day."

"Wedding day?"

A voice intruded into their moment—a voice she knew by heart.

Tate, dressed in charcoal tailored pants and a fitted yellow dress shirt, stood in the corner of the room. She hadn't seen Tate since she had left the intensive care unit, but that hadn't surprised her. He had said what he needed to say and they had nothing left between them.

"Matt asked me to marry him and I've agreed," Kate answered elatedly.

"Congratulations, Kate."

Kate rose from her chair and Chloe watched painfully as the two embraced. Was Tate thinking of his proposal to Kate? The one she had rejected? She couldn't read Tate's response, and any further conversation was cut short by another knock at the door.

Erin and Ryan walked in together, and soon her little room was full of people who all loved and cared for her, and she felt ashamed at the self-pity and jealousy she had been indulging in.

Erin had already been in earlier that morning, on her official morning rounds, but Chloe had gotten used to her checking in before she left for the day.

"I just came to see if you needed anything," Erin explained, her eyes fixed only on Chloe. Maybe she too felt the awkwardness of the Chloe-Tate-Kate love triangle.

"I'm good, thank you."

"When do you think Chloe will be discharged?" Tate asked Erin.

"She can be discharged tomorrow if she feels well enough to go. But she can't stay alone for the first few weeks."

"She can stay with me," Kate volunteered.

Chloe stared at her friend and knew she had been genuine with her offer, but she couldn't accept. Not with Kate's new engagement and her long overdue reunion with Matt. She wouldn't intrude on their time together.

"No, Kate, you need to be alone with Matt."

"Chloe, you are welcome to stay with me."

All eyes turned to Ryan, who didn't seem at all bothered by the surprise his offer had garnered. She was friends with Ryan, and he had saved her life, but she had never crossed that far into his personal life.

"I don't think that's a good idea."

Tate was glowering at Ryan, and Chloe felt her anxiety rise along with the escalation of tension in the room.

"Why not?" Ryan replied, his ease in contrast with Tate's decree.

"Because Chloe is still a resident and you are her attending physician."

Oh, God, had he really just said that? Didn't he remember that Kate had been a resident and he her attending physician throughout their entire relationship? She looked at Kate, who had made the same connection and seemed just as embarrassed by what they both knew was coming.

"Just because your intentions toward Kate were less than admirable does not mean mine toward Chloe are. Chloe needs a safe place to recuperate. I can provide that, no strings attached."

"I agree with Tate." Erin's voice interrupted the men's discussion.

All eyes turned to her. Chloe didn't care what came out of Erin's mouth—she was just grateful the two alpha males had been interrupted before it had got ugly...or uglier.

"I don't think *you* are the right person to comment on propriety," Ryan rebuked.

If the room hadn't been quiet already, Ryan's remark would have sealed the silence. Ryan did not suffer fools lightly, but she had never seen him as confrontational as he had been with Tate and now Erin. The attack on Erin's personal life both surprised and disappointed her.

"*Enough*. I appreciate everyone's concern, but I am an adult, capable of making my own decisions and deciding what is in my own best interests. Erin, are you sure I can't go back to my apartment as long as I don't overdo it?"

Erin took a deep breath, seemingly shaking off Ryan's comments before turning to address Chloe alone. "Yes, I'm sure. With your low hemoglobin and naturally low blood pressure I think you are at high risk for dizziness and fainting and you shouldn't be alone."

Chloe couldn't fault her reasoning or her recommendation. The idea of waiting to be found again was terrifying. She looked between Kate, Ryan, and Tate, considering the three less than desirable options before her. She wouldn't intrude on Kate's happiness. So that left Tate and Ryan.

If Ryan hadn't just surprised her with his behavior she would have accepted his offer. She was used to rumors that she'd used her beauty and sexuality to advance her career—what was another log on the fire?—but she had no idea why he was so angry with Tate. And though it did not feel like romantic jealousy she didn't want to take that risk with someone who was going to be a long-term colleague once she became staff herself. That left Tate. But he hadn't offered despite his argument with Ryan.

She drew in a deep breath. "Tate, could I stay at your loft?"

No one said anything. Not Kate, not Ryan, not Erin, and definitely not Tate. She watched as her words penetrated through, with only a slight change in his eyes registering their impact. Finally he answered.

"Yes, it's the least I can do."

She almost gasped, fearing what he would say next. Was he going to declare to everyone he was the father of her pregnancy?

"Kate deserves some time alone with Matt to celebrate their engagement," he finished.

She was too crushed by his words to think about whether they had been genuine. It was still about Kate—it always had been. Would it be always?

True to his promise, Tate appeared again in her room the following morning, ready to take her home to his loft. She had spent a near sleepless night trying to decide if she really could live with Tate, and when she had slept her dreams had been torn between the pleasure and the pain she had felt the last time she had been at his loft. She had finally given up and showered and dressed early, wanting at least to feel like herself before facing him. Her black tights fit her comfortably and provided support for her abdominal wall, and the red cable sweater dress felt soft against her skin and made her feel more feminine that she had in days.

She had gotten used to the appraisal that accompanied his visits.

"Have you been discharged?"

"Yes."

"Okay. Let me get a wheelchair and I'll get you out of here."

"I don't need a wheelchair."

"Chloe, you cannot even walk once around the unit before needing to sit for a break. So your options are a wheelchair or I carry you—pick."

The image of being held in his arms and carried through the hospital reminded her of the finale in a romantic movie and she was momentarily lost in the vision. Then his other words sank in. He likely had not just guessed at what her activity tolerance was, he had been checking up on her. It both pleased and annoyed her.

"Wheelchair, please."

"Not as much fun, but okay."

She was taken aback by his return to humor and she smiled too as he left the room to get the chair.

Her smile was brief, and it faded as Tate pushed her through the hospital halls. She watched as nurses, residents and other physicians did double-takes at the sight of them together. She had always garnered some attention, but had never been bothered by it until now. She had always been able to take comfort in knowing that she was more than what people saw and that their perceptions were usually not the truth. This time there was the high likelihood that no matter what indecent scenario they were imagining between her and Tate the truth was a lot worse.

She stopped looking and focused on her hands, folded in her lap. She still had bruising from the numerous intravenous lines and her hands were as pale as the rest of her.

"Everything okay?"

Tate's voice sounded from above her.

"I'm fine."

"You don't seem fine."

How had he noticed her discomfort without even looking at her?

She wanted him to keep moving so she needed to reassure him that she was physically okay and not about to be sick or faint from the chair. "I'm uncomfortable with people staring."

"I thought you would be used to it by now."

"Why would I be used to people staring at me?" she asked defensively.

"Because you're gorgeous, but you don't let that get in your way. It intrigues people."

She wanted to know more. To know how else he saw her. How he felt about her. But she didn't know what else to say so she raised her head and squared her shoulders as they finished their journey toward the parking garage.

Erin and Tate had been right, though she did her best to hide that particular truth. Once at his building the walk from the main entrance to his loft door was too much. She wanted to sit, or at least to lean against something, as a now familiar wave of dizziness threatened to make the choice for her. She needed help and it was a hard truth to swallow.

"Dammit, Chloe," she heard as a strong arm snaked around her, pulling her up to rest against Tate's strong frame.

She barely noticed him unlocking and opening the large steel door before she felt another arm reach under her legs as her feet left the floor and she was carried inside.

"I can walk," she protested.

"Sure."

The soft weave of his couch was soon under her, and the loss of the heat from Tate's body was replaced with the weight of a soft chenille blanket that covered her whole body and the glow from the fireplace. She wanted to close her eyes, but was instantly aware of the green eyes at face level with her own as Tate bent beside her.

"Enough with being strong, Chloe. I know I'm not your favorite person right now, but you need to learn to ask for help."

"Why do you say that?" She wasn't angry with him and hoped he didn't think she was. She was just frustrated with the situation they found themselves in.

"Because it doesn't do anyone any good to take unnecessary risks."

His words struck her. Tate was a risk, but to her he felt necessary. "Why don't you think you are my favorite person right now."

"Because I'm responsible for your pregnancy."

"You are not the only person responsible, Tate. I was there too. And if things hadn't turned out this way I would have been happy about the baby." She was out on a ledge, letting him know how she felt. Did he feel the same way? "Do you want children?"

"Yes. It was one of the reasons I wanted to get married."

"To Kate." She finished his sentence, not wanting anything left unsaid between them. She also noticed he'd used the past tense. Had the loss of Kate eliminated marriage and children from his plans?

"Yes, it was one of the reasons I proposed to Kate," he admitted. "I didn't realize you and Ryan Callum were so close."

It was a question disguised as a comment. It was also a way to change the conversation. She decided to let him. Discussing his past relationship with Kate was too painful.

"He's my mentor."

"He invited you to stay at his house." The same approach, the same hidden question.

"I think my collapse scared him," she answered honestly.

"He's not the only one."

"Why?" she asked honestly. How could he profess to have felt scared when he had not wanted anything to do with her in the weeks prior?

"Why what?"

"Why were you scared?"

"Because I care about you, Chloe. Surely you know that." His words flooded through her and she felt both warmth and annoyance. How would she know he cared about her when he'd walked away from her and never looked back?

She couldn't let it go. "You stopped speaking to me after we slept together." She tried to leave her pain out of her words and focused on the facts.

"That wasn't because I didn't care."

"Then why?"

She watched his frustration as he ran his fingers through his hair. "Because I'm not good for you, Chloe."

"Don't you think I should be the judge of that?" she asked searching his eyes for an answer.

"No, I don't." He rose up and walked away, signaling the end of their conversation.

Despite the cost and quality of his couch there was nothing that was going to make this night comfortable. He resisted the urge to shift again, taking penance in his discomfort. Even if he had been in the world's most comfortable bed it was unlikely he would be able to sleep. Not with Chloe so near.

He had had weeks to think about how they had gotten to where they were now. He had been weak—that was how. He had meant what he said to her: he wasn't good for her.

Chloe—of all the women to take to bed. Months of sleeping alone, licking his wounds and trying to restore his pride had definitely blurred his boundaries. It wasn't just that a woman had wanted him; it was that *Chloe* had wanted him. He had had his choice of woman since he was fifteen, but she was different. He respected her. She was capable and strong and an amazing physician. She was also a dedicated friend. Most importantly she was Kate's best friend.

Up until a year ago his professional life had been his only life. He had relentlessly pursued his career, moving through each step with ruthless succession from his degrees from Ivy League institutions with honors to the top residency and fellowship programs in the country. By the time he was in his mid-thirties he was one of the top ten vascular surgeons in the country, recruited with a large salary and various other incentives by one of the top tertiary centers.

He hadn't gone without women during that time. He enjoyed sex—it was like operating, a series of movements and responses that led to the culmination of something intensely satisfying. But the women he'd chosen knew the score, and while he'd respected them, and what they offered, he'd felt no other emotion toward them.

Then he'd met Kate. He hadn't intended to become romantically involved with her. He had started as her mentor within the Department of General Surgery, helping her hone her skills and making sure she had the right opportunities and surgical cases that would allow her to grow as a surgeon and show others what she was capable of. She had quickly exceeded his and everyone else's expectations and their relationship had transitioned to friendship.

Being around Kate outside of the hospital, outside of work, had opened his eyes to what he wanted in a woman. He didn't want a woman whose entire life's ambition was to gain her "Mrs." He was looking for a partner who would stand beside and challenge him, as opposed to the old adage of the "woman behind the man." Kate had seemed like the logical choice, so he had pursued her with the same intensity he had his career.

Never in his life had he failed at anything. He knew when he was going to win, and when something was a losing proposition, but not with Kate. He had asked her to marry him and she had said no. As a man who had never failed he hadn't taken it well. But all the anger he had felt at the time now felt completely misplaced. He shouldn't have been angry with Kate for refusing him. He should have been angry with himself for pursuing her at all. What had felt like all the right reasons had been anything but. He hadn't been in love with her.

How had he expected to live a life of intellectual companionship, mutual respect and admiration with no spark? No heat? A poor decision that he'd thought was behind him was now front and center. His past relationship with Kate was going to ruin any potential future with Chloe. How could he expect Chloe to see him as anything other than Kate's past?

Chloe. His mind had a reel of images of her. Chloe trembling with his touch. Chloe beneath him, losing control. And Chloe lying on an operating room table almost dead. The catastrophic result of their night together should have been enough to end any attraction to her, but it hadn't. Emotionally he had no idea how he felt about her. Physically he wanted to touch her, to comfort her, to be one with her until everything about them made sense.

CHAPTER FOUR

SHE FELT COLD. She brought her knees up and curled on her side, only to be rewarded with a pain that spread throughout her abdomen. She could hear screaming, followed by yelling, but she couldn't tell what was going on and all she could see was black. She concentrated hard on opening her eyes, and when she did everything else disappeared.

She grasped the sheet to her, feeling more vulnerable than in the cold of her dream. She struggled to slow her breathing and calm herself as she took in her surroundings. The sheets were not hers. The room was not familiar. In an instant she remembered she was at Tate's.

"Are you okay? Can I get you something or help in any way?"

His voice projected across the loft and with a moderate effort she was able to push herself up and see him. He was seated at the breakfast bar, drinking from a coffee cup, his laptop in front of him. His attire was casual, no suit or tie. He wore a sweater in warm cream and designer jeans.

She glanced at the bedside clock. It read ten in the morning. How had she slept for that long? Wasn't it also a week day?

"You are not at work?" She stated the obvious.

"No, I'm working from home."

"Tate, you are a vascular surgeon. How do you work from home?"

"I canceled my elective cases for the next two weeks and have arranged for my on call to be covered."

"You didn't need to do that."

"Yes, I did. I know you, Chloe, and I can't trust you to take things easy. If you are still at high risk for dizziness and fainting than you shouldn't be alone. That means whether you are at your place or mine."

She wanted to argue with him, embarrassed by what she knew to be the colossal sacrifice he was making, but she couldn't. Her near collapse yesterday and her fears of something bad happening to her with no one around to help circumvented any argument.

"Thank you."

She moved toward the edge of the bed and before her feet hit the floor he was at her side.

"I'm okay."

"Prove it."

She looked at his face, freshly shaven, at his green eyes, clear with one eyebrow raised, and knew that there was no way he would be backing down. She was surprised that she found herself feeling more honored and protected than annoyed.

She managed to move to a standing position—the physical task she had found the hardest and the most painful since her surgery. Once on her feet she moved toward the bathroom, Tate inches behind her. As she passed through the bathroom doorway she stopped and turned around toward him.

"Happy?"

"I wouldn't go that far, but you did great."

A look at his face confirmed his words. Of course he wasn't happy—what was there to be happy about? She had invaded his life and he was now being forced to care for her. She should be grateful, and she forced herself to reserve her feelings of sadness until she was truly alone.

"Thank you. Now, if you'll excuse me...?"

"Leave the door open."

"What?" she questioned, shocked by the request. The bathroom was her only possibility for privacy. She hadn't yet had a chance to see what she really looked like post-op, and wanted some time alone to finally see the scar that would forever remind her of what she had lost.

"The bathroom has a separate toilet and door for privacy, but if you are going to be in the shower with hot water and prolonged standing I'd like you to leave the door open so I can hear if you need me."

"Is that the only reason?" she teased, needing to lighten the conversation and her thoughts.

"I have a photographic memory Chloe. I can see you naked any time I want. Go shower. I'm here if you need me."

For the next four days they didn't leave the loft. She slept and studied, and spent more time talking to Tate than she had in the years prior. She knew a lot from the time they had spent together while he was dating Kate, but now they had the opportunity to talk just the two of them and she loved their conversations. They talked about everything—their families, their past, their education and career plans—and Chloe really began to feel as if she truly knew him.

She was reading a textbook chapter on abdominal pain when the front door buzzer rang. Tate didn't appear surprised and buzzed the person up without speaking. There wasn't time to ask questions as he made his way to the front door.

Her mouth fell open as he met and greeted an older woman. With her classic silver-gray bob and the same height and eyes as Tate Chloe knew it was his mother. She immediately tried to make herself presentable, adjusting the cream cowl neck sweater she was wearing and trying desperately to rein in her hair, which she had left to tumble freely past her shoulders.

The pair made their way to her and she tried to stand, but the pain and tightness she still felt in her abdomen slowed her.

"Oh, dear, please stay sitting," Tate's mother admonished thoughtfully.

Tate smiled, and she couldn't help but share his sentiment.

"Mom, this is Chloe Darcy. Chloe, this is my mother— Lauren Reed."

She reached out to shake her hand but instead was enveloped in a warm embrace.

"Lovely to meet you, Chloe. I'm so glad to hear that you are doing well."

An overwhelming feeling of being cared for overrode her thoughts about what Lauren Reed knew. Had Tate told her about the pregnancy? If he had she seemed unconcerned with their circumstances.

"Thank you, Mrs. Reed."

"Oh, please call me Lauren."

"Thank you, Lauren."

"I asked my mom to stay with you while I run some errands this afternoon."

Chloe blushed, both at his thought and at his mom being asked to be her "babysitter." "That's not necessary."

"I knew you would say that—that is why we both agreed not to mention it to you. I'll be back in a few hours. Have fun."

Had he really just winked at her? Chloe made a conscious effort to keep her jaw from dropping as she watched Tate grab his jacket and keys and leave.

"Can I get you a cup of tea, Chloe?" Lauren offered.

"Yes, please." Truthfully, she would have preferred something stronger as she had no idea how to handle this new setting.

She watched as Lauren moved through Tate's kitchen with obvious familiarity. She knew Tate was close with his family, but it was still lovely to see how close as his mom effortlessly put together a tea service and returned to sit beside Chloe.

"Thank you for the tea, and for taking the time to spend with me today."

"It's my pleasure, Chloe. It is not often my son needs me these days, and I appreciate the opportunity to meet the reason why."

She was still smiling, and Chloe got the feeling there was a lot she was not saying.

"I appreciate everything Tate has done for me."

"Well, don't appreciate my son too much. We both know he has his faults, and he needs to be reminded of them every once and a while."

"Excuse me?"

"Tate's stubborn and independent. It's been great for his career but not for his personal life."

If Chloe hadn't already been surprised by the day's events, she would have been shocked now.

"Don't get me wrong, dear. Your friend Kate is a lovely girl, but she wasn't right for Tate. She didn't inspire him. My son needs to be challenged. Tate needs to be uncomfortable."

It seemed as though Tate's mother knew more about their dynamic than she had thought. Chloe's mind replayed all the ways she had made Tate uncomfortable. From the aftermath of their first and only night together to his nightly attempts to sleep on the couch. If her goal was to make him uncomfortable then she had succeeded.

"Mrs. Reed—" she started, before noticing the reproachful elevation of one of her companion's eyebrows. "Lauren," she corrected herself. "Tate and I are not in a romantic relationship."

"It saddens me to hear that, my dear, but I have faith that it won't stay like that for long."

"I'm not sure…"

Lauren placed her hand on Chloe's and she paused mid-sentence.

"Chloe, I know my son well and I trust him. You should too. Now, enough with this seriousness—tell me more about you."

Two hours later Chloe was laughing so hard she thought she might need to restart some of her pain medication to deal with the soreness in her stomach. It was nice to have the lingering uncertainty of her relationship with Tate lifted for a short time. It was also nice to get to know Tate even more through the stories his mother told of his childhood with three younger sisters.

The front door of the loft slid open and Tate came through, with a bouquet of flowers in one hand and the other a collection of shopping bags.

He smiled at them both as he moved to join them, putting down his collection. "I see you two have done just fine without me."

"I was just telling Chloe about the time you were so desperate for a little brother you cut Emily's hair and insisted we all start calling her Eli."

"Not my finest moment," Tate acknowledged, with an obvious pride in his former self's ingenuity.

"Well, Chloe. It was wonderful to finally meet you and get to spend the afternoon together. I look forward to doing it again sometime soon."

"You are welcome to stay for a while, Mom."

"I know, Tate, but truthfully I came to visit Chloe—

not you. Now, if you'll excuse me, I'll leave you two as I found you. Take care of her, Tate. She's worth it."

Chloe felt herself turn the shade of her hair as Lauren once again embraced first Tate and then her, prior to leaving the loft.

"I would ask what you talked about while I was gone but I'm too afraid of the answer." Tate grinned.

"She's wonderful, Tate. You are lucky to have her— and so close by."

"I know. Even if she *does* have the habit of involving herself in my personal life."

Chloe felt herself blush, thinking back to Lauren's words about her son. She hoped she was right about Kate, and that Tate had come to recognize that too. She looked back at him and the collection of goods around him.

"Do I need to put those in water?" she asked, looking at the bouquet of brightly colored flowers.

"I can do it. I want you to open the rest first."

She stared at the large pile of packages and realized Tate had gone out shopping for *her*. "I don't know what to say…"

"Don't say anything—just open."

The first bag contained her favorite line of bath products. Bubble bath, shower gel and lotion, all in her favorite citrus and sandalwood scent. She looked up at him questioningly.

"I thought you deserved to smell like *you*."

She didn't know what to say, so said nothing and moved on to the next package. She pulled out the largest bag of wine gums she had ever seen. She looked up at him again, with the same surprise in her eyes.

"What you like to eat while you study."

Without response she moved to the third bag. It contained a collection of designer yoga pants, long-sleeve tops and hoodies. He answered this time before she could ask the question.

"I thought you deserved to be comfortable and knew these were your favorite."

She got to the last bag, only to discover high-waisted cotton underwear—granny panties. She was horrified and tried to stuff them back in the bag. She couldn't even look at him this time.

"Those won't rub on your incision," he explained, almost as embarrassed as she was.

Truthfully, her low-cut briefs had been rubbing painfully, but how he knew that she had no idea. She was touched by his thoughtfulness. Few men would be caught dead making this kind of purchase.

"Thank you."

They both stood and reached for the flowers. His hand closed over hers and for a moment stayed there as they met each other's eyes. He was so close she could smell the masculine scent of his soap—the one she had shared for the past few days. She wanted him to kiss her, but he didn't.

"I'll get you a vase if you want to arrange the flowers."

"Okay," she managed.

They both made their way to the kitchen and she unbundled the bouquet and set about trimming the stems. She started opening drawers in search of kitchen scissors when she saw it—a square light blue ring box. She wanted to put it back, to shove it to the back of the drawer and never look at it again. But she couldn't. Instead she slowly opened the lid to discover a diamond ring. She didn't have to think for long about what it was and who it was meant for. It was the ring Tate had bought for Kate—the one he had proposed with. But why had he kept it?

"Careful with that."

Tate's voice cut through her thoughts.

She felt like a kid caught with her fingers in the candy drawer. Without thinking she reached out and handed it to him. She watched as he closed the box and replaced it in the drawer.

"You kept the ring?" she finally managed.

"Yes."

"Why?"

"I have my reasons."

She could tell by the look on his face and his tone of voice that he didn't want to discuss it further. She did. His answer told her nothing. Did he think Kate was going to change her mind? Or did he want a reminder of their past together. How did he feel about Kate?

But all the questions that Chloe had in her mind were going to remain that way. Their conversation was definitely over, and Chloe was not going to get any of the answers she was looking for.

CHAPTER FIVE

AFTER TWO WEEKS Tate returned to work and Chloe welcomed the privacy. She needed to regain her independence, and that wasn't going to happen if she was constantly attended to by Tate.

A knock on the loft's industrial door snapped her from her train of thought. She put down the resuscitation algorithms she had been reviewing and braced her abdomen, using her other hand to steady herself as she made her way to the door. Kate, dressed casually in jeans and a light purple fitted shirt, was on the other side, with a new glow about her. She was beautiful, and for the first time in her life Chloe felt self-conscious next to her. She looked down at her black yoga pants and loose-fitting blue sweatshirt and knew she paled in comparison. Jealousy hinted at the edge of her consciousness and she did her best to push it away.

"Hi, stranger."

And Kate's familiar smile washed away any negative thoughts she had been feeling. Kate embraced her gently before they both moved back into the living room.

"How are you feeling?" Kate asked.

"Tired, sore," she replied. *Confused*, she added to herself. "On a happier note, how are things with you?" she added, needing to change the topic. She had had enough time to think about her own life recently.

"Wonderful. It's funny that for so many years I thought this would be the worst time of my life, with exam stress and getting ready to leave, but instead it is the best. Matt found a new apartment for us in New York to start our new beginning together, and we've decided to get married in the Hamptons on the August long weekend."

Kate's smile was infectious, and despite her problems Chloe felt a similar wave of happiness pass through her. A sparkle caught her attention and she immediately wondered how she had missed it. On Kate's left hand was a large emerald cut diamond flanked with two smaller similar side stones on a polished platinum band. It was stunning.

"Oh, Kate, it's so beautiful—and absolutely perfect for you," she gushed with emotion.

"I know. Everything feels right for the first time in a really long time."

Chloe's envy returned full force.

"Are things weird, living with Tate?"

Chloe was unprepared for the complete change of focus. She looked into her friend's soft gray eyes and knew there was nothing behind the question—and certainly no knowledge of what had happened between them.

She tried her best to put on the same smile she had for the past two years when talking about Tate. "Tate's been very generous, letting me stay at his loft and taking time off to stay with me. I'm very grateful."

She watched a flicker of doubt cross Kate's face she knew she hadn't sold Kate on her feelings. She was happy when Kate let the matter drop.

"And Ryan?" Kate asked.

Chloe was surprised again by the question, and the change in Kate's tone and facial expression as she asked about the other man. She looked even more serious than when she had been discussing her and her ex's living arrangements. On the other hand things *had* been weird that day in her hospital room, and Chloe herself wasn't as confident as she once had been in her perception of the other man.

"Ryan's been great. He's called a couple of times, and next week he is going to come over and help me practice some oral examination questions for the Boards."

"Is it awkward, seeing him?" Kate asked.

"Because of the pregnancy?" Chloe asked, her confusion still present.

"Yes."

"It was at the beginning, but Ryan has been really discreet and understanding about everything that happened and we are moving past it."

"Do you think you will be able to work together still?"

"Yes, definitely. We are both professional adults, and both very good at our jobs, so it shouldn't be hard. Probably easier than *your* plans to come back here to work in the same department as Tate, the man you were almost engaged to, once you are done with your fellowship."

She didn't mean to sound defensive but she knew that she did. It was just hard to imagine that on top of everything her relationship with Ryan had also changed.

"I guess… My relationship with Tate seems like a lifetime ago."

"It was nine months ago," Chloe corrected.

"Yes, but things are so different now, and we have both moved on."

"Kate, he professed his love for you and asked you to be his wife."

"He didn't mean it."

"How can you be sure?" Chloe asked. Her heart was still convinced that Tate was hung up on his Katherine.

"Sure of what?"

"How do you know Tate is over you?" Because *she*

certainly wasn't over them, and she wasn't convinced Tate was either.

The slide of the heavy loft door ended their conversation as they both directed their attention to the man walking through it. It was one of his rare daytime appearances at home and Chloe had to wonder how much it had to do with Kate's visit. He did, however, seem surprised at his ex's presence.

Kate stood from the couch. "Hey, I just came over to visit Chloe."

"I can see that. You are welcome anytime, Kate."

"Thanks."

The exchange held no tension but it was still painful to watch. Tate tossed his keys into a bowl at the front entry and removed his suit jacket, draping it over one of the chairs in the living room before coming to sit with them. Chloe felt herself running her fingers through her hair before she was aware of the action. She sighed audibly; nothing was going to make her close to Kate's beauty—not at this moment, and maybe never in Tate's eyes.

"Are you tired? Do you want us to leave so you can rest?" Tate asked, his attention focused on her.

"No, I'm fine."

Two pairs of eyes looked at her skeptically.

"Really, I'm fine. I'm not used to doing nothing, and it's hard not to be able to do the things I used to do."

"Like...?" Tate asked, and she hoped she didn't seem ungrateful for everything he had done for her.

"Go outside," she said. She felt as if she was going crazy, being alone all day with nothing but her own thoughts, but she had promised Tate she wouldn't go out alone.

"Let's go out, then. If you want we can go out for

dinner tonight. Somewhere close by and familiar, but still *out*."

"That would be great," she agreed, her outlook already improving.

"Kate, would you like to join us?" Tate asked.

She looked at her friend expectantly, willing her to say no.

Kate repeated Chloe's words. "That would be great."

"Then it's settled." He pulled off the tie that had been knotted at his neck and undid the collar of his shirt before proceeding into the kitchen to make arrangements.

Chloe stood again and made her way toward the bedroom platform, opening her designated drawer and searching for something that would both fit and be flattering. She managed to settle on a previously loose-fitting royal-blue jersey dress that now clung to her still swollen breasts and the curve of her hips. It would have to do. Her brief pregnancy and the post-operative changes to her body had ruled out the majority of her wardrobe.

She gathered the uncontrolled waves of her hair into a ponytail and used what little make-up Kate had packed to add some color back to her face. When she was done she knew it was an improvement, but nothing compared to Kate.

When she exited the bathroom she found Kate and Tate both on the couch. The quiet conversation that they'd been having was immediately stopped by her presence. Maybe she was wrong—maybe things *could* become more uncomfortable between her and the two people she loved most in this world.

She put on the same smile she had for the past two years. "So, where are we going?"

"Kate suggested Italian."

"Sounds great—let's go."

* * *

The small restaurant was familiar, and a comfort to Chloe. She hadn't realized how isolated she had felt until she was out. The *maître d'* hugged and kissed both women affectionately before shaking Tate's hand, recognizing him on sight. "Dr. Reed we have an excellent table for you and your companions this evening."

"Companions" was a safe descriptor, Chloe thought as they were led to a curved booth that had already been set for the correct number. Tate grasped her arm as she gently lowered herself down onto the leather. He didn't follow, and Kate entered the other side, moving to the center as Tate sat opposite her.

The first few minutes were filled with silence as they all examined their menus and selected their meals.

When the waiter returned Tate ordered a bottle of red wine and appetizers for the table and they each ordered.

"I was hoping you were going to pick the steak," Tate commented after the waiter had left.

"Why would I pick the steak?"

"To help replace your iron."

"Is that why your housekeeper keeps preparing meals and stocking the fridge with red meat, leafy greens and fortified cereals?"

"Maybe," he answered, with a small satisfied smile on his face.

Kate's laugh broke through and Chloe couldn't help but join in.

The *maître d'* arrived with their bottle of wine, uncorked it, and offered a small amount to Tate for his approval. Once approved, he began filling glasses. Chloe declined, not sure how the wine would affect her ongoing nausea and mild dizziness. The *maître d'* filled Kate's glass and paused mid-pour, his eyes fixated on Kate's ring.

"Congratulations, my dear. I didn't realize there was cause for celebration. Dr. Reed has magnificent taste in both women *and* rings."

Chloe felt her mouth fall open and her eyes widen in horror at the man's assumption. He obviously knew Tate, and had known them both as a couple. She looked at Kate, who looked equally as uncomfortable and speechless.

"Thank you, Antonio." Tate graciously accepted the intended compliment with no obvious embarrassment.

Chloe watched as Antonio left, still speechless. Had that really just happened?

"Well, he is right on at least one account." Tate remarked as he took a large sip from his glass of wine. "Beautiful ring, Kate."

She wondered if he was comparing it to the one *he* had bought for Kate.

"Thank you. We've set a date for the August long weekend in the Hamptons. I hope you can come."

Chloe looked over at Kate, who was fidgeting nervously, turning her ring round and round on her finger.

"I wouldn't miss it."

How was it possible that *she* was the most uncomfortable with this conversation? But, looking between the two of them, she realized she obviously was. Thankfully the conversation changed to work, and Chloe breathed a sigh of relief. Then their appetizers arrived, followed by their main courses.

They talked about the hospital and the upcoming Board exams. Tate and Kate even briefly asked about each other's families, and Chloe couldn't get over the level of comfort and how at ease they were with each other after everything. Times had changed, it seemed—not just for Chloe, but for Kate and Tate as well. She wasn't sure which scenario she was more comfortable with: Tate and Kate not speaking to each other immediately post-breakup, or this back-to-normal resolution.

She looked down at her plate of seafood linguine and realized that she had barely touched her pasta. It tasted amazing, but her appetite was still not back and the ever-present feeling of nausea she had struggled with over the past few weeks still had not subsided.

"Are you okay?" Tate asked, his eyes directed at her full plate.

"Yes," she answered. "I just haven't gotten back to my regular appetite yet."

"Has this been too much?" Kate asked.

Yes, she thought to herself. Not the outing and not the meal, but the combination of the three of them together felt like too much.

"I'll get the check and take you home."

Before she could answer Tate had signaled for their waiter, who presented himself promptly.

"That's not necessary. You two should stay and enjoy your meal. I can get a taxi."

"No, I'll take you home." Tate was resolute, and she knew not to argue the matter further.

"I'm sorry," she apologized to Kate.

"Don't be. It's normal to still be exhausted by the little things. It will get better, I promise." Kate reached out and squeezed her hand reassuringly.

They drove back to Tate's loft together, dropping Kate off at her car before entering the underground car park. Once back inside, Chloe felt spent.

"Are you going back to the hospital tonight?" she asked, not knowing what his new routine would be but hoping for some privacy to digest the evening.

"No. I thought we could relax and watch a movie together. If you fall asleep that's okay too."

She was taken aback by the normalcy of his suggestion. They really didn't *do* normal. They did passion and distant and awkward to a tee.

"That would be great. Give me a few minutes to change out of this dress and wash my face."

"Sure."

She walked back toward the bathroom and changed into loose-fitting shorts and a T-shirt. It wasn't exactly the finest lingerie, but it was what she had with her and it covered her body and eased her self-consciousness. When she emerged from the bathroom most of the lights were off in the loft and the television that was stowed within one of the tall bedroom cabinets had arisen from its hidden resting spot. She was surprised to see Tate on what she thought of as "his" side of the bed, still fully dressed and on top of the covers. He had not moved from the couch or even approached the bed in the past weeks.

"I thought you would be more comfortable lying down than with both of us on the couch."

"Thank you." She moved slowly up the two stairs onto the bedroom platform, watching as Tate pulled back the covers as he had done once before for her, waiting for her to join him. He had placed some extra pillows on the bed to support their upper backs and heads.

"Do you have any preferences?" he asked as he used the remote to turn on the large flat screen.

"Something funny; nothing serious or violent. I don't need any more nightmares." She yawned.

The television went to "mute" and Tate turned to face her. "You're having nightmares?"

She regretted her words almost immediately. She'd been having nightmares even before her collapse and hospitalization. Her dreams had become much more vivid and she had become much more sensitive to the stimuli around her. Now, after her collapse, it was worse and she would frequently have dreams of patients she couldn't save. Sometimes that patient was herself and sometimes it was her lost baby.

"Yes."

"Do you want to talk about them?" he asked gently.

"Is it okay to say no? I already feel tortured enough during them; it's hard to think about them a second time."

"Of course."

The volume returned to the television and within a few moments he had selected a famous animated children's film, featuring a fiery redheaded princess heroine.

"I thought you would appreciate something familiar."

She turned toward him. No sound escaped him, but she could see from the subtle movements coming from him that he was laughing silently at his own reference. She smiled at this return to his trademark sarcasm.

He smiled back. "Truly, Chloe, my sisters and my nieces all swear it's a great movie for both children and adults."

"We'll see…" she said, in the same teasing banter.

She wasn't sure when she nodded off, but it was a deeper sleep than she had achieved in the past two weeks. And Tate didn't leave her for the couch.

The first time she stirred she felt a strong arm cross over her and his soft words echoed through the darkness. "You're okay." This happened several times through the night, until she was welded against him the way she had once been. Somehow she remained conscious of where she was and her dreams of helplessness remained at bay.

After that evening she was never alone. She didn't dare question how he had managed to avoid nights on call for a total of four weeks now, but instead relaxed into the solace he provided. Every night he would sleep next to her—fully dressed and on top of the covers she was tucked beneath, but next to her just the same.

She feared she was growing dependent on him. She needed to remember that this was not permanent and that once she was recovered they would go their separate ways.

She pushed away the textbook she had been reading and stood. She was feeling better and better every day, with her incision pulling only slightly at the corners and her nausea subsiding.

She walked to the bathroom, which had soon become her favorite room in the loft, both for its privacy and its luxury. She stripped from her clothing and entered the shower. She would miss this shower. The large glass enclosure was imposing, but also comforting. The showerhead had multiple settings, perfecting the pressure of the hot water that sprayed all over her body.

The sound of the shower water was one of the few that could drown out her thoughts. She stood until the heat began to overwhelm her senses and threatened to interfere with her still precarious balance. Dense steam covered the mirror and filled the room, which preserved her solitude as she made her way to the large double sink and mirror. She wiped the excess water from her body and wrapped a towel around her before she started on her hair. She worked through the long red waves as best she could, soon tiring and taking breaks between sections, letting her body weight rest against the counter.

She felt a hand cover her own before she saw him. The shock led to a small gasp and the final loss of her balance. She reached out to the hard granite for support. Unfortunately in the process of doing so her loosely slung towel fell to the floor.

"*Oh, God,*" she thought, and was surprised to hear her voice expressing the sentiment.

"No, just me—Tate." Tate, quiet and sarcastic.

She smiled and just for a moment forgot that she was standing in front of him completely naked. She started to bend for the towel, but was beaten to it by Tate, who had already bent to retrieve the lost covering.

He stopped midway in rising. Chloe didn't dare to look down and instead closed her eyes. He was at eye level with her lower abdomen and she felt his hand trace the incision that now ran along the top of her bikini line. Despite the fact that he had already seen her naked, had already been deep inside her, this felt more intimate than anything prior. His face was very close to her most private of areas and she was completely naked under his fully clothed assessment. He placed his hand flat against her abdomen and she could feel him through the numbness she had acquired. His hand slid upwards but stopped short of her breasts, which she felt his eyes appraising even though she still couldn't bring herself to look.

She finally opened her eyes as she felt the towel being fastened securely around her. Apparently he found her lacking, and the sting of rejection burned throughout her body. She had barely glimpsed his face before he grasped her shoulders and turned her toward the mirror.

She remained silent, transfixed at the slow appearance of her reflection as the steam cleared from the mirror. Tate took the brush from her hand and worked it through her long hair, gently teasing away the tangles with his fingers and being careful not to pull at her scalp. It was hard not to melt into the moment. His actions were intimate, but his earlier evaluation and rejection kept her tense. He didn't look up from the task at hand until he was finished, and then his face rose to meet her gaze through the mirror's reflection.

"When is your follow-up appointment?"

The words surprised her and a chill coursed through her body.

He walked away from her briefly, returning with his robe. The black terrycloth was warm and heavy on her shoulders as he helped her thread her arms through the too-long sleeves. She appreciated the physical barrier.

"When is your follow-up appointment with Dr. Thomas?" Tate asked again, and she was just as surprised by the question on its second asking.

"Next week. Why?"

"I'll have to rearrange my schedule."

"That isn't necessary. I can take a cab."

"I want to be there."

"Why?"

"I have some questions."

"What's happened has happened and nothing can change that."

"I know."

His acceptance surprised her. "So what is the point, Tate?" Her frustration was breaking though.

"I need to know that you are going to be all right."

"I am." She needed to believe that even more than she needed *him* to.

"I'm still going."

"Be reasonable, Tate. My appointment is at the hospital. How is it going to look if people see us together?"

"I could care less."

He meant it. Maybe it was ego, maybe it was confidence, or maybe it was just that Tate Reed's love life had been the center of the hospital rumor mill for so long that he really didn't care. But she did. She had learned not to let the rumors about her supposed love life faze her, but the thought of the hospital being abuzz about her picking up where her best friend had left off was too much.

"I care."

"You shouldn't."

"There are a lot of things I shouldn't care about, but that doesn't change the way I feel, Tate."

"I'm sorry."

She turned from the mirror to look at him directly and she could see the truth behind his words. He *was* sorry. Sorry for *her*. She could only fear why. Did he know about her feelings?

"It's not your fault." It wasn't. Hadn't she always known where his heart lay?

"Isn't it?"

She couldn't continue this. "No, it's not. I think I should move back to my apartment."

"I'd like you to stay until after your follow-up appointment with Dr. Thomas."

"I don't think that is a good idea."

"When has *anything* between us been a good idea?"

It was him again—same old Tate—and even if his words were true they still hurt.

"Never," she conceded.

"Then why break our pattern now?"

"Because this isn't normal, Tate. We're not a couple and we cannot keep acting as though we are."

"Is that what you think I've been doing? Acting?"

His eyes had narrowed and she immediately felt as if she had said something more hurtful than she had intended.

"No, Tate. You've been great the past few weeks. But this isn't who we are, and I can't keep relying on a combination of your generosity and guilt to make you take care of me. I need to stand on my own feet again."

Surprise and discomfort were apparent as he tensed the features of his face and withdrew slightly from her. "It's not like that."

"It's exactly like that. Up until my hospitalization you wanted nothing to do with me. I understand why, and appreciate the change of heart, but this—us—isn't what you had planned."

He looked as if he wanted to argue the matter further but no words left him as he stared at her.

"I'll drive you home when you're ready."

"Thank you." A sense of relief she hadn't known she was holding in left her as Tate finally turned and left the bathroom. She watched him, waiting for the door to close behind him, but he stopped and turned back toward her.

"Chloe, I still intend to be with you at your appointment next week." The door clicked shut behind him.

So maybe they were not completely done.

CHAPTER SIX

SHE LASTED THREE days at home before she truly thought she was losing her mind—or would if she didn't go back to work. It wasn't just the isolation at Tate's apartment that had been getting to her, it was the complete departure from her previous life that she couldn't stand. She loved and needed her work. It was the part of her normal life which she had been searching for most desperately.

She was more nervous about her first day back at work than she had been for her first day of residency. But she walked into the emergency department and her nerves eased. The familiar hum of the department felt like home.

She went to change into her scrubs. The women's change room was not any different, despite the fact that she had almost died on the floor. She shuddered and walked quickly to her locker, pulling on the dark blue top and pants, annoyed that she still had some postoperative swelling in her abdomen, making the pants more snug than normal.

She entered Section B—minor treatment—and smiled. Standing at the triage desk was Ryan Callum, and she appreciated the familiar face.

"I didn't know you were on today," she remarked casually, wanting things between them to remain as they always had been.

"Apparently some of us don't know when to stay home. Welcome back, Chloe."

He was smiling at her but she could still feel his concern and assessment.

"Thank you—for everything." She knew that was all that needed to be said between them.

She went to grab for a chart when the sound of a child's wailing pierced through the department. The sound wasn't new, or even out of place in the Emergency Department, but there was something about this particular cry.

She found her answer in the red face of a toddler who was being held down by one of the other residents in an attempt to establish an intravenous line. It wasn't a cry of pain, but a cry of terror. There was a nurse, but no other people in the room—no parents. The child looked terrified.

"Dr. Russell?" Chloe called, and both the resident, Andrew Russell, and the child paused in their battle to focus on her. "Can I speak to you for a moment?"

She could tell he was angry but she didn't care. She didn't say a word until they were outside the cubicle with the sliding door shut.

"Yes, Dr. Darcy?" Dr. Russell's tone was unmistakably bitter.

"What is that child presenting with?" she asked, not rising to his confrontation.

"How is that any of your business?"

"Andrew, what's wrong with that child."

"I didn't realize you were back. Must be nice to get five weeks off. I wonder what entitled you to special treatment? Come to think about it, I don't need to think about that one very long." He looked leeringly down toward her chest.

"Dr. Russell, I suggest you regain your professionalism before you say something you will regret. Now, what is wrong with that child?"

"You won't be Chief forever, Chloe."

"No, you are correct on that. As of July first I will be attending staff at Boston General—so, as I said, Andrew, don't say anything that you are going to regret."

She watched as disbelief and then resignation passed over him. She knew that she was the only resident to be hired direct from training in the past ten years and if Andrew had any hope of ever returning to Boston General he had to keep himself in line.

"She's a three-year-old who fell from two and a half meters in height at daycare. After the accident she was somnolent and unresponsive and now is combative and irritable. I'm trying to establish an intravenous so she can be sedated for a CT scan of her head." His arrogance had returned.

"Why are you doing a scan?"

"For the reasons I just explained."

"But look at her now. She is very oriented, responsive, and quite frankly terrified."

"That doesn't mean she doesn't have a brain injury."

"I agree. But what I disagree on is exposing a three-year-old to potentially scary treatment, not to mention unnecessary radiation."

"So what do you suggest I do?"

"Call Pediatrics, ask that the child be admitted for observation, and find her parents. That is what she needs."

"Will there be anything else?"

He knew she was right, but that didn't change the animosity between them.

"Dr. Russell, I guarantee that when you present your new plan to Dr. Callum and the pediatric attending you will be commended for your conservative management. Why don't you go do that?"

She watched as he walked away before she went back into the cubicle. The little girl focused on her and she watched as her little chin began to wobble and tears filled her eyes. Chloe moved slowly, choosing to sit next to the little girl and doing her best not to intimidate the already frightened child.

"Hi, sweetie, it's okay to be scared. No one is going to hurt you."

The little girl was still eyeing her suspiciously. She looked between Chloe and the nurse, her fear still very apparent. The nurse was still holding the intravenous supplies and looming above them both.

"Cassie, we're good here."

The nurse took her direction and left. The little girl instantly relaxed and Chloe left silence for a few minutes. She watched, rewarded, when the little girl slowly scooted down the bed toward her.

"Do you want to go and play with some toys?"

She nodded and held out her arms, waiting to be lifted. Chloe reached for her and hoisted her into her arms, swaying slightly at the weight of her and the unexpected difficulty of the task. She steadied herself and then made her way out of the cubicle toward the pediatric play area.

"Jaclyn!"

Chloe swayed for a second time as the little girl jerked in her arms. Chloe turned in the same direction, to see a woman running frantically toward her. When the woman reached them the little girl jumped from her arms and into her mother's.

"Oh, thank God," the woman cried. "How is she? Is she all right?"

"She's much better now. We've asked a pediatrician to come and see her, and possibly admit her overnight for observation, but I think she is going to be just fine. You can wait with her over in the pediatric play area, if you like."

"Thank you so much for taking care of her."

"She's easy to take care of."

Chloe watched as the woman walked away, with the little girl, Jaclyn, still holding her tightly. A mother and her child. *She* wanted that. She had assured Tate that she was going to be all right, but that didn't mean she hadn't spent the last five weeks worrying. Would she ever be a mother? Would she be able to have a successful pregnancy after everything that had happened? Would she find another man she would love and whose child she would want to have?

She shook away her thoughts and went to grab another chart.

Four hours later she was exhausted. She had spent the day suturing, casting and following up tests, but she felt spent despite the simple treatment needed by her patients.

Chloe rested her head on her hand as she scrolled through the computerized images that had sliced her patient's abdomen into sections for review. The radiologist had reviewed the same images and attached a report, but she always looked first. Finally she saw it: the inflammation in the patient's right lower quadrant and the swollen prominence of the appendix. It wasn't a surprise. Her exam had already made the diagnosis, but confirmatory imaging made it an easier sell on consultation.

Ryan joined her at the monitors. "If you already knew it was appendicitis why did you get the CT scan?"

"Because a CT scan clearly demonstrating appendicitis will get the patient to the operating room faster than asking General Surgery Service to take my word for it. This way they can take one look at the images and book the patient instead of a medical student, then the resident, re-examining the patient and maybe still ordering a CT scan because they don't trust their own exam skills and are too scared to be wrong."

"So it was easier to expose the patient to unnecessary radiation and expensive testing than to argue your findings?"

He was challenging her, as he always did. She should be grateful that he wasn't going easy on her.

"Today it was," she admitted, her usual sense of fight replaced by the exhaustion her first shift back had created.

"I think your plan has backfired," Ryan replied, looking up with a new coolness in his voice.

She raised her head to look in the same direction and met Tate's eyes staring across the department at her. He was wearing scrubs and was accompanied by one of the general surgery residents and a medical student.

"The entire team appears to be here to discuss and evaluate your patient."

Tate strode toward them, his focus clearly on Ryan. "Ryan."

"Tate."

She immediately knew things were still hostile between them. Both men were behaving out of character and a spirit of antagonism radiated between them.

"I was surprised to hear that Dr. Darcy had a consultation for our services. I would have thought the Emergency Department would have been a little more accommodating," Tate commented, his criticism lacking any veil.

"The Emergency Department has always been supportive of Dr. Darcy in all the professional choices she makes—including her decision to return to work."

His emphasis on the word *professional* was making it clear to both of them that he didn't support the recent personal choices she had made.

She looked at both men and knew she needed to end this before something was said aloud that she didn't want said. The general surgery resident was clearly uncomfortable with this deviation from the norm. Having his staff come downstairs to supervise a basic appendicitis consult was demoralizing. And the medical student didn't seem to know any better.

"The patient is a twenty-four-year-old woman coming to the Emergency Department with a one-day history of increasing abdominal pain that has now localized in the right lower quadrant. It hurts her to move and she is lying very still. She has nausea and vomiting associated with the pain and no other symptoms. On exam she is febrile, with a pulse of one hundred and thirty, and blood pressure is normal. She has rebound pain, guarding and tenderness over McBurney's point on exam. Investigations show an elevated white blood cell count of eighteen thousand and normal hemoglobin, electrolytes and kidney function."

She relayed the history, providing all the relevant information for the benefit of the medical student, trying to transition the discussion back to medicine and teaching.

"Ask Chloe why she ordered a CT scan on such a clear-cut case," Ryan said.

Tate's eyebrows were raised at her. He was not willing to play directly into the conversation Ryan was orchestrating. The gesture was as good as the question, though.

"I ordered the CT to definitively prove appendicitis." She waited, knowing that Ryan was not going to be satisfied with her response.

"Chloe was just arguing that General Surgery will no longer take a patient to the operating room based on history and exam alone, no matter how classic the presentation."

It was said as a challenge, from one department to another, about how they provided patient care. It was also an escalation of a testosterone-fueled dispute she would have never predicted from either man.

"I don't think it best practice to make assumptions about what *any* service would or wouldn't do. Dr. Munnoch, please go and consent the patient for surgery and discuss aspects of informed consent with our student."

The resident and the medical student left.

"Chloe, can I speak to you for a minute?" said Tate. It was less of a question for her and more a direction for Ryan to leave.

"Okay," she affirmed to both men, and waited for Ryan to go before choosing her next words. "What are you doing here?" she asked, as patiently as she could manage.

"I was going to ask you the same thing," he replied, his annoyance even more clear in the absence of observers.

"I'm working, Tate. This is where I work."

"I don't have a problem with that, Chloe. Where and with whom you work is none of my business."

"What is that supposed to mean?"

"Ryan Callum is very protective of you."

"Ryan Callum has always been there for me and he helped save my life. Surely if anyone can understand the relationship between a mentor and a protégée it's you?"

Her temper had gotten away from her and she regretted her words even as they met her own ears. Drawing a comparison between her and Ryan and Tate and Kate wasn't fair, or accurate. There was nothing romantic between her and Ryan.

"This isn't about Kate," he replied defensively, not missing the undercurrent of her remark, but his voice only carrying as far as her.

"*Everything* is about Kate," she stated, knowing it was the truth between them.

"That's far from the truth."

They were getting nowhere. "Tate, what are you doing *here*?" she asked again, as a means to end their conversation's previous trajectory.

"I agreed to take some General Surgery on call to make up for my recent absence. I was surprised to hear from my resident that *you* were the consulting physician. I wanted to make sure you were okay to be back at work."

"You don't need to worry about me. I can take care of myself." For the second time that day she felt a clinical appraisal as Tate's eyes ran up and down her body.

"We'll see about that. What time are you done?"

"I'm just finishing up. The appy was my last patient."

"Page me when you are done and I'll drive you home."

"That isn't necessary," she replied with frustration.

She understood where Ryan and Tate were coming from with their protective overtures, but enough was enough. Despite everything that had happened she didn't doubt her own capabilities, and they shouldn't either.

"That wasn't an option, Chloe. I'm either driving you home to your apartment or my loft. Those are your options."

It wasn't worth the fight. When had she ever been able to change Tate's mind about anything? "Fine. I just need to sign off the chart and change."

She walked away and back toward the change room, discarding her scrubs into the hospital linen basket and getting back into her own clothing. Her jeans were even more snug than they had been that morning, and they dug uncomfortably into her lower abdomen.

After thirty seconds of discomfort she gave up and undid the button and the zipper. She retrieved a hair tie from her pocket and threaded it through the buttonhole, using the loop end to secure the button a few more inches away from where it had previously been fastened. She untucked her white button-down dress shirt and slipped on tall brown leather boots over the skinny legs of her jeans before leaving.

"Everything okay?"

Tate's voice greeted her before she'd even realized he was standing outside the women's change room door.

"Didn't anyone ever tell you it's creepy to stand outside women's change room doors?" she replied, with both humor and aggravation.

"No, but—as I told you a few days ago—I really don't care what other people think."

Chloe Darcy was going to be the death of him—if she didn't bring herself to permanent harm first. He'd hated dropping her off at her apartment, and equally hated the sight of his empty loft. His love of the masculine open concept design had vanished and now the space felt large and empty. Unfortunately he was more than aware that what was bothering him most about the space was that she wasn't there.

When had what seemed so wrong—Chloe Darcy in his bed and his life—started to feel so right? It wasn't what he had planned…it wasn't even something he had pursued. Two words that had defined every achievement in his life: planning and pursuit. But Chloe had just *happened*, and he felt more insecure with her than he remembered ever feeling before. He had no idea where he stood with her, or if there was the possibility for anything more.

Had he ruined their chances by being with Kate? There were so many questions that needed to be answered. He couldn't read her. Except that since her hospitalization there was a new sadness about her that she tried to keep to herself. Was it the loss of the pregnancy? Or was there something more?

Ryan Callum was an unwanted facet to this situation. It didn't help, seeing them together. Even an outside observer could see that Chloe was clearly more comfortable with Ryan than she was with him. He had never in his life felt jealous of anything or anyone, and it was a new emotion he didn't enjoy. The sight of Ryan and Chloe together made him want to throw away everything he had worked for and earned in favor of a macho display of aggression he had never considered before.

Then there was Chloe herself. She was different, and something was telling himself to pay attention to those changes. He didn't know how but he had a definite feeling that there was something still linking them together.

CHAPTER SEVEN

SHE STILL HADN'T gotten used to being a patient. Sitting in the waiting room of Dr. Thomas's outpatient clinic, she thumbed through a magazine meant to help her pass the time until it was her turn. She had arrived ten minutes earlier, after getting blood work done, and now was both anxious for the appointment and about Tate's arrival.

She had managed to dissuade him from picking her up, but not from attending the appointment. It was funny that despite all they had shared and the personal nature of their acquaintance she was still uneasy about having him hear future predictions of her fertility. Being declared permanently damaged would be hard enough for her without knowing it was another way she wasn't good enough for Tate Reed.

"Chloe Darcy," a nurse called from the front of the clinic.

Chloe rose and followed the nurse to one of the examination rooms, turning with one last glance toward to the clinic's front door and breathing a slight sigh of relief at Tate's absence. She didn't know what had changed his mind, but she was grateful none the less.

She waited another ten minutes before Dr. Thomas entered the exam room. "You look better," the middle-aged man greeted her as he came to sit at the desk beside her.

"Thank you."

"How are you feeling?"

"Okay. I'm occasionally sore, but the incision has healed well. Still tired, and occasionally nauseated, but I am not sure how much of that is recovery versus my Board exam in two weeks."

Dr. Thomas's eyebrows rose as he wrote down some notes. "I remember those days well—you'll be fine. Did you get the blood work done?"

"Yes, about an hour ago."

"Okay, why don't you get changed while I go and see if the results are ready? I've paged Dr. Madden to come and see you as well. She'll be in to discuss the blood work and do the exam. There is a drape on the bed—everything off from the waist down."

She watched as he left and closed the door and then complied with his instructions. She slipped off her jeans, followed by the low-rise bikini briefs that fell below her incision, tucking them neatly into the folded jeans, then smiling at the idea of hiding your underwear from a person who was about to see you naked. She covered herself with the drape and waited.

The wait seemed like forever. Then a knock at the door sounded and she held her breath, still waiting for Tate's promised appearance. It was Erin Madden. The petite blond had achieved average height in heels and had her hair down, which was a rare occasion.

"Hey, Chloe. Dr. Thomas paged me to let me know you were in for your follow-up and asked me to come see you. It's hard to believe it has already been six weeks. How are you feeling?"

"Okay. Good days and bad days, I guess. I went back to work this week and that has helped. But I haven't been studying nearly as much as I planned and will be more than happy then this exam is done. I'm surprised to see you still at work. I would have thought you would have been off studying too."

Erin's face held the same hopeful and yet exhausted expression Chloe had come to recognize as the same look *she* had worn for some time.

"You know what they say about best intentions."

"Well, I'm here, aren't I?" Her usual humor was to cover the pain she still felt about the events leading up to her pregnancy.

"How are you feeling *really*?" Erin asked, pulling the stool from the end of the bed so she could sit and talk to her friend.

"Disappointed, frustrated—take your pick. It's hard to admit that I made such a mistake, both in getting pregnant and then not even having the medical sense to realize it. I want to be able to move past it, but I can't seem to get back to normal. I still feel tired, nauseated, and I have no control over my emotions, which just leads to more frustration."

"You may be being slightly hard on yourself."

"I know."

"Chloe, would it be okay if I examined your abdomen and we did a quick bedside ultrasound?" Erin asked, and for the first time in their conversation Chloe felt uneasy.

Something was not right.

"Of course. What are you not saying, Erin?" she asked while at the same time turning to lie on the examination table as Erin washed her hands and then moved the drape to sit low on her hips.

Erin didn't respond immediately, but her face was doing a poor job of concealing her thoughts. Chloe both felt and watched her friend's hands move over her abdomen, her fingers pressing flat two centimeters above her pelvic bone.

"Your blood work from this morning shows a persistently elevated beta-HCG."

"What does that mean?"

"It shouldn't still be elevated. If we had performed a salpingostomy and removed only the ectopic pregnancy than some residual placenta might be present in the fallopian tube, leading to the elevated hormone level, but…"

"But?"

"But your tube had ruptured and we were unable to control the bleeding from the rupture site, so we performed an open right salpingectomy, removing the entire fallopian tube. The pathology report confirmed the presence of the pregnancy. So your beta-HCG shouldn't still be elevated, unless…"

"Unless what?"

"Chloe, you may not be able to move on. I think you are still pregnant."

Time stood still as Chloe replayed the words in her head and waited for something in Erin's expression to clarify her statement.

"I don't understand."

"I think your pregnancy was a heterotopic pregnancy. One inside the fallopian tube and one in the uterus. It's a rare condition, occurring in only one in every five to thirty thousand pregnancies."

"How do we find out for sure?" Chloe managed through the pounding of her heart.

"We look."

And without further discussion Erin squeezed warmed jelly onto her abdomen and placed the ultrasound probe against her. She turned toward the screen that was visible to both women and watched as the clear outline of a baby appeared. She could see a head, body, a heart flickering, and legs and arms that stretched out and explored their environment.

"A baby…" she stated with wonder.

"Your baby," Erin confirmed. "I'm just going to do some measurements to date the pregnancy."

"There is only one date possible."

"Which makes you about fourteen weeks along."

"Does everything look okay?" she asked, her surprise over the baby being quickly replaced by fear that her surgery and the medication she'd received had caused her baby harm.

"As much as I can see right now, everything looks okay. but we're going to need to do some investigations. You received a lot of blood products that they initially didn't have time to match against your own blood screen. You also received some medication we don't recommend in pregnancy, but right now you have a baby."

"A baby…"

"How do you feel about that, Chloe?"

She watched the screen in awe. Both she and Erin were silent as the small figure moved around and she tried to reconcile in her mind the fact that everything she was seeing was actually happening inside her. She watched as Erin moved the cursor over the tiny flickering heart and was mesmerized by the sound of the heart beating that filled the room.

"Wonderful."

"Okay, so we will just go from here. I am going to give you a requisition for prenatal blood work and another ultrasound in four weeks' time so we can look at the rest of the baby's anatomy."

"Erin, is it weird that I am excited and terrified at the same time?"

"No, I remember that feeling well. You're going to be a wonderful mother, Chloe. Congratulations."

A mother…a baby…*her* baby.

Chloe felt the first genuine smile she had experienced in months turn the corners of her mouth as she got dressed, no longer frustrated at the swelling in her abdomen as she took a moment to rest a hand against it before finishing dressing.

"Hello, little one, I'm your mom and I love you so much already," she whispered aloud.

She grabbed the requisitions and left the examination room and the clinic before her first thought of Tate came to mind as she saw him striding toward her, still in scrubs and a scrub cap, with a look of irritation apparent on his face.

"I'm sorry," he greeted her before she had a chance to worry about her words to him. "Another team got into some massive bleeding and I got called in to cross-clamp the aorta."

"Don't be." Her joy was too much even to let the heartache of Tate bring her down.

"Can we go somewhere to talk?"

She wanted to tell him that they had nothing to talk about, but she now knew that was not true.

"Yes."

They walked together to one of the many coffee counters in the hospital. After getting a large black coffee for him and a peppermint tea for her they took the table for two furthest from the others.

"How was your appointment?" he asked.

She thought about the baby. She needed time to get used to the idea before she added the complexity of Tate into the equation. "It was good."

"So all your tests came back normal?"

Tate was looking at her expectantly. For a brief second she had the feeling that he knew her secret, but there was no way he could and she wasn't going to be pushed into telling him before she was ready.

"Yes," she answered simply.

She tried to tell herself that pregnancy was a normal state and she wasn't lying to him, but even she did not believe that.

"Tate, can I ask you something?" she started hesitantly.

"Since when did you need permission, Chloe?"

He was smiling at her and she couldn't resist smiling back. He was right. She was known for being direct and to the point. It was one of the things that made her a great emergency physician.

"Good point. What would we have done if the pregnancy hadn't been ectopic?"

He didn't answer her. Apparently it wasn't the question he'd been expecting.

"But it was," he said eventually.

"Yes. Pathology was returned confirming the pregnancy was in my right fallopian tube." The truth—which again felt like a lie.

"So why are we discussing this?"

She could hear the frustration in his voice but she wasn't going to back down.

"Because I'd like to know." Because she needed to know now that there was a baby growing inside her.

Tate sighed and for a moment she thought he wasn't going to answer. "We would have figured it out."

"What does that mean to you?"

"It means we would have done what was best for the child. Chloe, why are we talking about this?"

"Because it's something I think about. And I wondered if it was something you think about too. The 'what if?'"

"No, Chloe. I haven't been thinking about something that was never a possibility in my mind."

She felt her face fall but in her mind knew she had no right to be hurt. Why would Tate think about the "what if?" He probably thought of her failed pregnancy as his narrow escape from a path in life that had not been of his choosing. *She* was the one who dreamed of their life together.

She couldn't tell him. Not today. She wasn't prepared to see the disappointment on his face when he realized that his lucky escape was no longer. Not when her heart was so full of love for the life they had created together.

He watched Chloe walking away, studying her every angle and movement. There were very few occasions when he resented his job but today was one of them. It had been a life or death situation that had kept him from attending Chloe's appointment, and now he had to live with the consequences.

He had wanted to be there with her. He knew she was afraid of the possibility of permanent damage and he'd wanted to support her. He'd also wanted to assure himself that she was okay and going to be okay long-term. Her nightmares had scarred not only her but him too. He already had the image of her on the operating room table burned into his mind, but her nightmares had added the sounds of her whimpering and fear to the mix too.

What *would* he have done if the pregnancy had not been an ectopic? He honestly didn't know. So many of his feelings toward Chloe had grown from the threat of losing her. If he hadn't faced that threat would he feel the same?

She floated through the next two weeks. Everything that had been challenging her dissolved into the background as she embraced her pregnancy and the prospect of motherhood. Every pregnancy symptom became a welcome burden, reminding her of the life growing deep inside her.

After spending five years preparing and living in fear of her Board exam she walked into the examination hall with full confidence in her knowledge and abilities. Eight hours later her confidence was still with her as she arrived at Kate's apartment with their long-standing plan to celebrate together still in place.

She climbed the stairs, smiling at the new effort it took. Kate opened the door with a smile too, and she knew that her friend had done as well as she had expected her to. She really was both brilliant and a gifted surgeon. They hugged tightly before Chloe walked through the door.

"Where's Matt?"

"He had a hearing in New York that couldn't be rescheduled, so we are going to get together this weekend to celebrate. But he *did* leave this in the fridge!" Kate revealed a bottle of very expensive champagne tied with a large bow and a note.

"Are you sure that is not meant for your weekend together?" Chloe asked, smiling at the gesture.

"The note reads: 'Congratulations, Kate and Chloe, I never had any doubts. Love Matt.' So, yes, I am sure." Kate worked her way through the kitchen, opening the bottle with a flourish designed for champagne and pouring two fluted glasses. She raised her glass and Chloe mirrored the action. "To achieving everything we want and to the happiness we deserve."

She clinked her glass with Kate's and brought the glass to her lips. It wasn't until she had the briefest hint of the crisp liquid on her lips that she remembered she shouldn't drink alcohol.

"What's wrong? Is it horrible?" Kate asked, her concern evident.

"No, it's not that. I'm sure it's wonderful. Kate," she started, realizing there was no turning back. "Kate, I'm still pregnant."

Her friend's eyes reached their widest dilation before they fell from her face to her abdomen. "I don't understand. I thought it was an ectopic pregnancy?"

"It was—but it is also an intrauterine pregnancy. Twins, in a sense."

"Oh, my God. How pregnant *are* you?"

"Sixteen weeks."

"Wow!"

She watched as Kate processed her disclosure and a large smile came to her face.

"Is it okay to be happy and excited for you?"

"It's perfectly right. I'm happy for me too. And excited—and scared."

"Did you tell the father?" Kate asked, her voice tentative.

She looked at Kate, waiting to see if there was any judgment in her face. She was sure that Kate did not know about her night with Tate. There was no way Kate would have held that information inside. But just now Kate had said "the father" as though she knew who that title referred to. Maybe she had been more transparent in her feelings than she had thought.

"No. I only found out two weeks ago, and I needed some time to get used to the idea myself. And I wanted to get past the exam."

"But you *are* going to tell him, right? I mean there is no way you can avoid the issue and work at Boston General."

"I know—but not today and not tonight. Tonight is about us, Kate. And congratulations—you are going to have to drink for two!"

Her cheer was genuine, and also meant to take them back to their original purpose and away from the thought that had not left her head in two weeks.

"As my first official duty as Auntie Kate, I couldn't be more honored. Now, let's get ready—we have a party to attend."

* * *

"Congratulations, Chloe, you look amazing." That was the comment that followed her throughout the night.

She wasn't sure if she had truly done *that* great a job, selecting the emerald-green cocktail dress with a deep V front and back and aside gathering that hid the changes to her figure, but she was gracious none the less. She knew people were genuinely happy for her—especially in light of her well known brush with death.

She was happy too. She was spending the night celebrating with most of the residents she had worked with for years in her program and in other specialties. This was the end of an era and the beginning of her real life.

The party was being held at a local pub located near the hospital and frequented by the staff. Once a year it closed to the public for this celebration, and the familiarity of both the location and the people made it the perfect choice. In the background music filled the space, and the lights were turned down, adding to the atmosphere of the evening. She visited, she danced, and she discreetly avoided the celebratory drinks that were being passed around.

"I'm probably not the first, but can I tell you exactly how amazing you are and how proud of you I am, Dr. Darcy?"

She turned and smiled back at Ryan, who was standing behind her, holding two fluted glasses in his hands. "I couldn't have done it without you."

"You could have done it anywhere, with no help at all. I'm just happy you trained here and are staying here."

"Thank you," she said, and reached up to hug him carefully.

He handed her a fluted glass. "A toast to Dr. Chloe Darcy—a friend, an inspiration, and now my colleague."

She smiled and clinked her glass against his. As she

pulled her arm away she both saw and felt a hand close over her own on the stem of her glass. She recognized the hand, and didn't need to turn to see the man attached.

"Let's dance."

Not a request—more like a caption for Tate's intentions as she felt herself being relieved of the glass and pulled toward the dance floor.

"What do you think you are doing?" she asked, trying to make herself heard over the music but not by the surrounding dancers.

"I could ask you the same question," he replied, his tone matching his actions.

"I am celebrating, and I don't appreciate being barged in on and hauled away when the mood strikes you."

Her last words had been louder than she'd wanted as the loud music faded away and a slow song filled the room. She moved away, wanting the conversation over. But once again she was pulled back, this time finding herself pressed against Tate, with his hand pressing into her low back, pressing her to him, while his other hand still held hers tightly. Her bare skin pressed against dark denim jeans and the linen of his button-down shirt.

"And here I thought you would be appreciative," he drawled, but there was no ease in his words.

"Why would I be appreciative?" she questioned, her position such that she was staring just over his shoulder, her eyes unable to meet his.

"I didn't think you would want to drink alcohol," he whispered, his words soft against her ear.

His implication caused the complete opposite effect in her. She felt her back straighten and arch as she turned to face him.

"It's not good for the baby," he said.

She wanted to run—to do everything she could to avoid a conversation she was not ready to have—but any thought of that was lost as she felt Tate's hand and arm securing her to him once more.

"How did you know?" Her voice cracked as the words passed her lips.

"You just told me."

"Tate…" she beseeched him.

"You're different. I noticed a couple of weeks ago that the changes were not all post-operative."

"What do you mean?"

"A few weeks ago, in my bathroom, I noticed a new curve to your hips and your breasts appeared fuller. Pregnancy has definitely added to your perfection."

Heat coursed through her as she remembered his appraisal in the bathroom that day. Maybe he hadn't found her as lacking as she had thought. "We shouldn't be having this conversation."

"Shouldn't we? When were you going to mention the pregnancy? Or is it none of my business?"

"Not here," she implored, her eyes once again not able to meet his.

"Then let's go."

He didn't wait for an answer and with the same force hauled her off the dance floor. He didn't stop as they made their way through the pub, out through the front door and to his Range Rover, where he held open the passenger door.

She couldn't think about speaking until they were driving. She hadn't even said goodbye to Kate.

"Where are we going?"

"We are going to finish this conversation," Tate answered.

In no hurry to start talking, she said nothing.

She wasn't surprised when they arrived back at Tate's loft. If she'd been going on the offence she would rather do it in her own territory as well. He held the door open and she walked through the entrance, stopping in the middle of the living room and turning to meet Tate head-on.

"Now what?" she asked, exasperated with the going-nowhere track they were on.

"This."

He walked toward her and for the second time that evening gathered her against him. This time their entire bodies met as he reached into her hair and held in her in place as his mouth came down on hers.

She couldn't have broken away even if she'd wanted to and she was not sure she did. Since their first and only night together this felt like the only way they communicated with each other—the only time they were in sync, the only time she was able to forget about everything that complicated their relationship and kept her from getting what she wanted.

She parted her lips, taking in the taste of him, and he took the opportunity she presented. She met his kiss, allowing him to explore her and taking no less from him. Her intensity increased with every touch of his tongue and she felt herself channel all her emotions, good and bad, into their exchange.

She heard the tearing of her dress at the same time as cool air met her back. The hands that had previously held her to him were now freely roaming her body, and areas that had been cool were now given heat from Tate's body, hands, and mouth. She felt a second tug at her dress as the straps were displaced from her shoulders and the bodice was pulled towards her waist.

She wasn't alone. The sound of buttons being released was followed almost instantly by the pressure of Tate's bare chest against hers. The slight friction created as he ground into her, with his hands still moving over her back while his lips and tongue caressed her neck, was torture for her newly sensitive breasts. Finally the two met as his large palm cupped her swollen breast and he brought the sensitive peak to his mouth. She gasped at the intensity of the sensation and Tate paused for a second, his eyes venturing away from his target to meet hers. The look they shared was almost as primal as the sensation she had felt moments before.

She whimpered as his hands left her breasts and roamed down the sides of her body. She felt her dress being hiked up to meet the gathering of fabric surrounding her waist. She felt his hands come beneath her, his grasp on her bottom firm, as he once again returned to her mouth with punishing drive. She was being lifted from the floor, her legs wrapping around Tate for support and for desire. She could feel him pressing into her, and the knowledge of everything he had to offer made her most intimate of places pulse with anticipation.

She clung to him as he carried her through the loft and laid her before him on the bed. She finally opened her eyes enough to watch him rid himself of the now torn linen shirt and the belt he wore. Like a predator he came down on the bed over her, his body brushing her but not pressing down on her.

Braced on his forearms, he tangled one hand in the layers of red hair that had fanned out over the white duvet. His face came down to meet hers, the green of his eyes even brighter than normal, before his mouth reclaimed hers. The depth and passion within his kiss made her wonder where she began and he ended. Only as she struggled for breath, her heart racing from the heat, did he leave her lips and once again begin caressing the breasts he had teased earlier.

He alternated his ministrations with hand and mouth, each movement more exquisitely torturous than the one prior. When he finally released her breasts she felt bereft—until she realized his intentions. She felt his lips trail over her abdomen, his tongue encircling her belly button, and then he moved lower as his hands worked the material of her dress higher, exposing her from the waist down.

She hadn't worn any underwear with the dress and nothing stood as a barrier between them. His hands once again reached for her bottom and he began his path of seduction again, starting at her knee and gradually working along her inner thigh, each movement and each touch causing her to naturally open wider to him. He opened her with his tongue and she barely held herself away from completion.

She glanced down to see Tate caressing her so intimately, with a look of enjoyment on his face that made her let go completely. He wasted no time, and the same torturous seduction that her breasts had endured came again as he tasted, suckled and stroked her core, each movement bringing her closer and closer to a cliff edge, higher than she had ever climbed.

Then with one final stroke she broke, her back arching as she cried out into the silence between them. But he didn't stop as she contracted beneath him. He kissed and stroked and kept her wanting him.

He returned to lie over her, his lips softly caressing her own. It took her a few moments to realize his intention.

"We're not done," she declared softly, her hand now roaming him as his had done to her, making its way toward the ultimate fulfillment.

"I don't want to hurt you," he gritted, not stopping her but keeping himself rigid above her.

"Then give me what I want," she replied huskily as her hand delved beneath the fabric of his jeans and boxer briefs to grasp him.

She saw the struggle within him before he moved away from her, stripping himself of his remaining garments, and finally ridding her of the remnants of her dress. His eyes stopped on the swell of her abdomen and her scar before he moved over her again. In a sudden smooth motion he rolled them both, allowing himself to be flat on his back and she above him. She understood his intentions and moved herself astride him, giving herself her first intimate view of his length. He was perfection, and she couldn't resist touching him to see if the feel matched the visual. He was both soft and wet at the tip, but everything beyond felt like thick iron.

"Be careful, Chloe," he warned, his face clenched in a combination of pleasure and agony.

She leant forward, her breasts once again brushing his chest, her face centimeters from his. "Why?" she purred, reveling at the new equality she had gained in their union.

"Because I've never wanted to be inside a woman so badly."

She opened her mouth to his as she rose above him and in one movement encased him within her. They both cried out, each sound muffled by the other's mouth. She felt so full it was impossible to imagine more pleasure. Then she began to move slowly, wanting to prolong what she knew would be the ultimate release. Tate's hands fell to her hips but rested there only as she controlled their pace and his depth. She watched him as his expression transitioned from rapture to intense concentration.

"Chloe, I can't hold on much longer."

"Then don't."

And she increased depth and pace, bringing herself closer and closer. She could feel him hardening further within her, hear small sounds and noises, and then finally the hands that had rested on her dug in as she lifted herself and then came down hard and deep onto him. Tate's cry and the feel of the warmth spilling into her propelled her to her own ending.

She collapsed forward, her body spreading over Tate's as he once again tangled his hands into her hair.

"Marry me."

His words cut through her afterglow.

There was no way she had heard him correctly. She pushed herself up onto her hands, not caring as both her breasts and her hair fell forward. He didn't look as if he was joking.

"I'm sorry?" she asked, stunned by all the events of the night, but none more than this moment.

"I think you heard me."

He lay beneath her with all the confidence of a man sure of an outcome. Given everything that had just occurred between them, she could understand how he had gained this impression.

"No." She shook her head, the only movement possible as shock still paralyzed her.

"You didn't hear me?" His eyebrows rose and obvious doubt shadowed across his face.

"No, I will not marry you."

Her words surprised them both, but it was Tate's look of anger that spurred her into movement. She pulled herself from his body and practically stumbled in her attempt to distance herself from him. Love Tate? Yes, maybe she always would. But the idea of marrying a man who didn't love her—that was a purgatory that even she couldn't endure.

She turned her back on him and scanned the room for what was left of her dress. The torn heap of fabric quickly reminded her that it was no longer an option.

She walked to his dresser and opened the top drawer, knowing it was where his extra scrubs were kept. Despite the changes in her figure she still swam within both the top and bottoms, but she didn't care. She moved to the couch and sat to fasten the straps of her shoes. She raised her head to meet long legs clad in denim before her.

"You're not getting away that quickly, Chloe. You have some explaining to do."

He was still shirtless, his jeans tugged on but unbuttoned. He was gorgeous—and very, very angry with her, despite the attempt he made to conceal it. She didn't care. In what world was she obligated to explain *anything* after his nonsensical proposal?

"*I* have some explaining to do? *You* are the one who proposed. *You* have some explaining to do!"

"You're pregnant, Chloe."

"I'm very much aware of that fact." She didn't rise from the couch, not sure she could stand on her suddenly weak legs.

"Do you have a better offer?" he retorted, his attitude as harsh as his intention.

"Say what you mean, Tate." She stood, the extra three inches of stiletto heel compensating for their difference in height and allowing her to look him in the eye.

"I don't think I need to," he replied, his lip curling with disdain at his implication.

"Oh, no, I think this time you really do."

He opened and closed his mouth. No words came through. She stood inches from him, refusing to back away.

"What do you want from me, Chloe?"

"I don't know—but not this."

"You're pregnant, Chloe. It's no longer about what we want."

"It's not 1960, Tate. A shotgun wedding is no longer the necessary next step."

"So you don't think a child needs a father?" he replied with equal derision.

"I didn't say that..." For the first time she felt defensive and less sure of herself.

"Think about it, Chloe. How are you going to cope as a single mother? You don't exactly have a nine-to-five job, or any of the maternity benefits that type of job would provide. What was your plan? To deliver and go back to work the next day? Between your student loans and childcare even your physician's salary would be tight. Unless, of course, you were planning to completely neglect your child and take extra shifts."

"I..." She was lost for words as she realized the truth behind his commentary.

"Chloe, we're not perfect. But deep down we respect each other—and there is at least one area where we are more than compatible." His eyes instantly darkened and confirmed his words.

He was right about pretty much everything. Would she do it? *Could* she do it? Sacrifice herself and her wants for her child?

She was lost in thoughts of the possibilities and didn't notice Tate walk away from her. When he returned he reached for her hand, and she felt before she saw what he'd pressed into it.

She was mesmerized at the site of the blue square box within her hand. It couldn't be—he wouldn't... Again, like a moth to a flame, she opened the lid slowly, praying for a different result. It hadn't changed. It was the ring he had bought for Kate.

She didn't need to see more. She closed the lid—but not before her rage bested the hurt she felt inside.

She heard the sound before she comprehended what she had done. Her hand throbbed after its impact with Tate's cheek, and both of them were stunned by her actions.

But the ring box still pressed into her opposite hand was enough to keep her from backing down from her outburst.

"No," she answered. "I'm not settling for second choice. Goodbye, Tate."

CHAPTER EIGHT

TWO WEEKS LATER she hadn't spoken to Tate—but she had confirmed everything he had said to her. She had checked with the Human Resources Department at Boston General and once she was on staff she would no longer be covered for any type of maternity leave. Physicians were considered self-employed, not hospital employees, and therefore not entitled to any employment benefits. She had also checked with her bank. Her student loans and her line of credit were average amongst her peers, but substantial compared to the average student. The debt would not wait for her return from maternity leave, and would require payments starting in three weeks' time.

She didn't have a lot of options. She could take a week or two off at the most and then would have to work a full-time schedule of sixty hours a week to cover her loans, living expenses and child care. The idea of leaving her newborn in the hands of stranger made her want to stay pregnant forever. At least then they could be together. She didn't have family money, or nearby support to rely on. She was an only child and her parents were both academics—college professors who had been in their forties when she was born, making them now in their seventies. They lived in Montana and visited at most once a year, their schedules still very much dependent on the academic calendar.

She was stuck, and she was going to have to ask for help. The question was from whom? Did she ask Tate for help, knowing that his help would not come without questions and conditions she would have to answer and give in to?

Or did she ask Kate, or more accurately Matt, for financial help, knowing it would be years before she would ever be able to pay him back? She had only known him for a short space of time and, while she was completely confident in his and Kate's relationship, she had already done enough with her involvement with Tate to jeopardize her friendship with Kate. Asking her fiancé for an inordinate amount of money to help her support the child she was having with her ex seemed more bold than even *she* was ready for. They hadn't discussed her child's paternity again, or the events leading to Tate's proposal, but it was likely only a matter of time before everything came out.

It was hard to be over thirty, a physician, and still feeling as stuck and confused as a teenager.

She looked around the waiting room full of pregnant women and didn't miss the fact that she was one of the few women alone. She hadn't told Kate or Tate about this prenatal appointment and ultrasound so she couldn't feel sorry for herself—she had made a conscious choice to come alone.

"Ms. Darcy," a nurse called from the doorway, and she followed the woman down toward the exam rooms.

She waited patiently, and was happy and relieved when Erin knocked and entered the room.

"Hey, I didn't know you were still around. I thought you would be taking the last of your holidays before your move."

A small smile crossed Erin's face and Chloe couldn't tell if it was genuine or if there was something else going on.

"Well, you know what they say about best-laid plans. I've declined the fellowship in California and will be staying on here at Boston General."

Chloe did her best to mask her surprise and instead focused on the positive. "So does that mean you are available to be my doctor for the entire pregnancy?"

"If you'll have me—then, yes."

This time the smile was genuine and Chloe decided to leave things alone. She knew only too well the value of privacy.

"You have a deal."

Erin sat down and started leafing through the papers that had accumulated in Chloe's chart. "So your official due date, based on conception and last menstrual period, is November ninth. Your infectious disease blood work all came back negative and you are rubella and varicella immune. Your most recent hemoglobin is low to normal range, so we should make sure you are staying on your prenatal vitamins and adding some supplemental iron."

"Okay."

"Chloe, the test that *did* come back abnormal was your blood type and screen. You are B negative, and the antibody screen came back positive for anti-C and anti-Kell antibodies."

"Which means...?" she asked, the easygoing nature of their interaction disappearing as fear set in.

"It means the baby is at risk for anemia."

"What do you mean, at risk?"

"The baby's total risk for anemia depends on its blood. To determine how much risk is present we need to do genetic testing of your blood type and the same genetic profile of the baby's father, to determine the odds of the baby having the affected blood type."

Chloe felt the bottom of her stomach hollow at the thought of asking Tate for anything in light of their last conversation. "Are there any other options?"

"The other option is to do an invasive procedure called a cordocentesis, which directly samples the baby's blood from its umbilical cord while it's still in utero. It has some significant risks, but it would provide us with definitive information about the baby."

"No!" she refused adamantly, her hand reflexively covering her abdomen…her baby.

"It wouldn't be my first choice either. So instead we need to test you and the father and then follow the baby with serial bloodwork and ultrasounds for signs of anemia and heart failure."

"Tate."

"Excuse me?"

"The baby's father is Tate Reed."

"I know," Erin acknowledged simply, with no judgment in her eyes or her voice. "Chloe, this isn't a paternity test. It's a genetic profile of your blood groups. We have to grow the cells over two to three weeks and then we use specific markers to look for the subgroup antigens."

"How did you know?" Chloe asked, surprised.

"Tate was in the operating room the night of your ectopic and I realized very quickly that his concern for you stemmed from something beyond friendship."

"From guilt," Chloe commented, still regretting the new nature of their relationship, which felt as if it was based solely on guilt and obligation.

"I didn't think so—but I don't have a great track record when it comes to men." Erin shook her head and then stood. "Come with me. We need to get you to your ultrasound."

* * *

She knocked at the industrial metal door and held her breath waiting for an answer. She hadn't called ahead and the doorman, recognizing her from her previous stay, had let her up—no questions asked or notifications made. She had no idea how Tate would react to her, but knew that she needed him.

The door slid open to reveal Tate, casually dressed in washed denim and a fitted ivory T-shirt printed with a graphic. He looked neither happy nor surprised to see her.

"We need to talk," she opened, as peacefully as she could muster.

"I don't think that is in dispute," he replied, his eyebrows raised, signaling the same skepticism his response portrayed.

He slid the door wider for her to enter. He didn't move, though, and she brushed against him as she made her way into the living room. His body was as cold as his expression, but *her* reaction was the opposite. Every part of her that had touched him felt like fire. She swept the hair off her neck and pulled down the hem of her tank top, trying to limit the heat.

Without words Tate walked to the kitchen and returned with a glass of ice water. They both sat down on the center couch.

"Just like old times," he remarked sarcastically.

"Tate—" she began.

"I'm sorry," he interrupted her. "I was out of line the other night with the ring. Apparently I don't handle rejection well and my temper got the better of me. I'm sorry, Chloe."

"I shouldn't have hit you. I'm sorry," she said, echoing his apology.

"I'm not sure about that."

His sincerity was clear in his eyes and she felt her defenses soften.

"I need your help," she opened simply, before she could change her mind. She watched him, waiting for a response. He was looking at her and she had no idea what he was thinking.

"I'm glad." He had misinterpreted her, and she felt guilty for the misunderstanding.

"No, Tate. I tested positive for two blood antibodies which may attack the baby's blood cells, depending on its blood type. We need to determine the baby's risk of anemia."

She had his attention and she watched as his eyes drew to her stomach. "What do you need?"

"Blood work. They need to do some genetic testing to determine the baby's level of risk."

His jaw flexed and she watched as his Adam's apple rose and fell with his swallow. "Okay—on one condition."

"Excuse me?" she asked, unprepared for the request.

"I'll get the blood work done *after* you move back in with me."

"Tate, you can't be serious."

"I'm very serious right now, Chloe. You want something from me and I want something from you. As you have clearly demonstrated your unwillingness to consider marriage, I'll settle for having you under my roof."

"Why?" she asked, not understanding his reasoning.

"You need me, Chloe. Not just for the blood work, but everything involving this pregnancy and the baby. You're just too stubborn to see it."

"But what about what *you* want and need?"

"Chloe, do you really need to ask that?"

She didn't as she watched his eyes trail down her body.

"And what if I say no?" she challenged, though her words held no power.

"You won't. I know you. You want what is best for this baby."

"What about Kate?" The thought slipped out before she could take it back. She wanted so badly to take it back.

"What *about* Kate?" he replied, not giving an inch.

"You proposed to Kate. You wanted to spend your life with Kate—have a child with Kate," she explained painfully.

"Yes. And I also proposed to you. So far I am zero for two."

"It's not the same..." she mumbled, lost for words.

"Yes, I think we can definitely agree on that point. Kate didn't slap me."

"How am I going to explain?" she wondered aloud.

"What is to explain, Chloe? You're pregnant and you need me."

"You really are serious," she finally acknowledged.

"Yes. Let me prove it to you."

She watched as he reached for his cell phone, which had been sitting on the upholstered leather coffee table that was before them. He dialled a number but she had no idea what he was doing or who he was calling.

"Hi, it's Tate. I wanted you to be the first to know. Chloe and I are together and she is going to be moving in with me permanently."

Together? Permanently? When had that become part of the situation? She watched as he listened to the response, still having no idea who he had called. His mother? One of his sisters? Her bewilderment increased as he passed the phone to her.

"She wants to talk to you."

"Hello...?" she ventured carefully.

"I don't know what to say."

Kate's voice rang clear through the telephone line. Guilt for her actions and her lack of disclosure to Kate pierced through Chloe as she turned to Tate for a brief instant to transmit her hurt. She couldn't look at him for long, though. She was too hurt and too angry. The phone still pressed up to her ear, she walked through the loft and into the bathroom, where she shut the door.

"I'm so sorry, Kate," she apologized, and waited.

"You have nothing to apologize for, Chloe."

"Don't I?" she asked.

"No. Tate and I finished a long time ago. Chloe, is Tate the father of your baby?"

"Yes," she confessed.

"Wow, I didn't see *that* coming." A pause lingered, but Kate was still there.

"I'm sorry."

"Stop apologizing."

She could hear Kate's frustration, but she didn't know how to respond other than with her remorse. Instead she said nothing.

"Chloe, are you happy?"

"I'm overwhelmed, Kate—with everything."

"That's not surprising. Is there anything I can do?"

"Be my friend."

"Done."

They were going to be okay, and she was grateful for the one part of her life that was both stable and solid. "Thank you."

"You know it does make sense—you and Tate."

Chloe would have laughed if she hadn't felt like crying. "I think your new-found love and happiness has impaired your judgment."

"We will see. Are you at Tate's now?"

"Yes."

"Are you hiding in the bathroom?"

"I wouldn't use the term *hiding*, but, yes."

"Good luck, Chloe. I have the feeling you are going to need it."

"Thanks."

As she heard Kate hang up she wished she hadn't. She was torn between relief over the conversation she just had and anger at being forced into it before she was ready. She took a few minutes to gather herself, using a cold cloth on her face and neck to cool the combined heat of pregnancy and anger.

When she left the bathroom she found Tate in the kitchen, leaning against the granite countertop.

"Are you satisfied?" she asked, but her voice lacked the energy she needed to continue this conversation. She hadn't realized how emotionally exhausting it had been, worrying about Kate's response to her paternity time bomb.

"Yes. You look tired."

He hadn't risen to her accusation, and she did acknowledge that he lacked any hint of smugness or victory.

"Thanks. I *am* tired. In case you haven't noticed I've had a lot on my plate lately." She reached back and rubbed at her aching neck and shoulders.

He strode through the living room toward the couch, but didn't sit. "Come here."

She was too tired to fight, and in truth she was exhausted, so she did as she was told. When she reached him he gently nudged her onto the couch, but didn't join her. Instead he walked behind her, and before she'd realized his intentions he had swept her hair to the side and begun to knead gently at the muscles she had been tensing in anticipation of this meeting.

She didn't want to relax, but she didn't have a choice. The conflict between them melted as he pressed and stroked down her neck and shoulders, his fingers finding their way into her hair and pressing at the trigger points at the back of her scalp, causing momentary discomfort and then complete resolution of the tension.

"Better?" he asked, his voice lower and more comforting.

"Hmmm..." she murmured, still deep within a new state of relaxation and peace that she hadn't found in weeks.

His hands left her back and were placed on her arms before she felt herself being lifted and guided across the loft. She was too tired to ask any more questions. Without comment she took direction and lay down on his bed. She felt Tate prop an extra pillow under her side, taking the pressure off her lower back. Then a light blanket covered her as he leaned down and kissed her lips softly.

"Sleep," he commanded quietly. "We'll figure everything else out when you are feeling a bit better."

Tate perched on one of the metal and leather bar stools that lined his kitchen counter, sipping a black coffee. In the distance he could hear the sound of Chloe's breathing. Every once in a while she stirred and he waited for the pattern to resume. He had chosen this spot at the counter because it was the only way to keep himself from watching her.

He had no regrets about his method of persuasion. She needed something from him and he had come to accept that he needed *her*. Chloe made sense. She was beautiful, smart, and he respected her intelligence. But what was driving him to resort to manipulation was the way they were together. In truth, she was the first woman in his life ever to drive him crazy. How else could he explain his behavior?

But he had been completely out of line with the ring and didn't deserve her acceptance of his apology. He had kept the ring for the simple reason that it was too humiliating to return an engagement ring and admit to anyone other than himself his stupidity and resultant rejection.

He had never in his life been anything less than honorable in his treatment of women, but everything about Chloe made him willing to compromise his principles. He craved her, he wanted her, and no matter what she was going to be his and no one else's.

His initial fears about her reputation suffering from an affair between them were gone. He and Chloe were not destined for a short-term affair. All the fears he'd had of falling for her and losing her had vanished with the confirmation of her ongoing pregnancy. Their child would forever link them to each other and he would never let her get away. He knew he could make her happy and that they could have a wonderful life together, if only she would let them.

He heard a muffled song and tracked the intrusion to her purse, moving quickly to silence the call. The display flashed back at him: Missed Call. Ryan Callum.

It was interesting how falling for a woman could change a man. His initial feelings of jealousy toward Ryan were now more than familiar. He knew there was nothing romantic between them, but he hated it that that night Ryan had saved her when she had been calling for *him*. Hated that she trusted Ryan and turned to him when she needed to talk. He didn't like thinking of anyone having a closer relationship with her than he did—romantic or not.

He looked over and saw Chloe had moved only slightly and then resumed her rhythmic breathing. He placed her phone back in her purse and then noticed the envelope that had been nestled beside it. The logo was Boston General's Fetal Assessment Unit's. The baby. *His* baby. He opened the envelope and looked through the stack of pictures inside. He wasn't ready for the black and white images that flashed back at him. Feet, hands, heart and a profile of the baby's face were featured on the ultrasound images.

He sat on the couch, overcome by the feelings the images evoked in him. This was their baby. This was the person that he and Chloe had made together. He searched the pictures for details. The baby had his nose. He wanted to see more. He wanted to know more. He looked back at Chloe, but he couldn't wake her.

His conversation with Chloe replayed in his mind. It was a high-risk pregnancy—not only because of the initial ectopic but also because of the anemia. He already felt he couldn't lose Chloe, but now he felt that way about their child. He needed to do everything he could to support her and decrease any stress in her life. Despite his method, that was one of the many reasons he wanted her back under his roof.

She had asked him to get the blood work done and he would—for her. Chloe had called it "genetic testing"—in a kind euphemism for a paternity test—but he knew what she really meant. He understood her need to get the test done. She needed to prove to him that he was the father. It was unnecessary, but he was willing none the less if that was what she needed. He would do anything for her.

She had always loved her work, but now it had truly become a refuge. Tate had given her two weeks to finish her residency, organize her life, and then he expected her to be with him. She would have thought she wouldn't be nervous about living with him—she had already done so for four weeks—but this time things would be different. He had been clear about his expectations. They would be a couple in almost every sense of the word, with the exception that she still had no idea how he felt, other than that their attraction was still present and burning hotly between them. She couldn't help but think that his desire to be with her was just related to their baby, and that if there was no baby there would be no them.

It seemed that her life, which had felt out of control for

the past four months, was going to continue to be so. But she had no regrets. She had their baby's best interests at heart. It had begun to move in the past week, and every flutter or stir overwhelmed her with love. She would do anything for the little person growing inside her, and if there was a possibility that her being together with Tate would provide a more stable home for their child, she would do it.

Now she was working her last shift as a resident and she wished it would never end—a stark contrast to most of her training, when she had often *worried* that it would never end.

She glanced through the charts, looking for something to take her mind off her impending fate. Chest pain—perfect. Her heart hurt too.

She walked to Critical Track Room Three and began her assessment. "Ms. O'Brien? I'm Dr. Darcy."

The patient, a forty-one-year-old woman, stared back at her, her eyes wide, her face displaying the panic she was feeling.

"Everything is going to be okay," she reassured the woman, taking a seat on the stool beside the bed and placing a warm hand on the woman's clammy arm. "When did this start?"

"About two hours ago," the woman replied, her voice breathless. Clearly she was not able to answer in a single breath.

Chloe glanced to the monitors and noted oxygen saturation of eighty-five percent and an elevated pulse of one hundred and twenty. "What are you feeling now?"

"I can't catch my breath, and there is a gnawing pain in the middle of my chest that hurts more when I take a deep breath."

"Have you ever had anything like this before?"

"No."

"Do you have any medical problems?"

"No."

"Surgeries?"

"I broke my leg a few weeks ago and they had to fix it in the operating room."

Chloe focused her attention on the woman's lower body, which had been covered by hospital blankets. She made sure the room's curtain was fully drawn before uncovering her legs. The left leg was in a cast, and above the cast the skin was swollen and reddened. She pressed behind the knee and the patient pulled her leg away in response to the pain.

"When did your leg starting hurting more?"

"A few days ago. I just thought I had overdone it."

"Are you on any medication?"

"Just some over-the-counter pain medication and my birth control pill."

"Any allergies?"

"No."

"Okay, Ms. O'Brien. We are going to start some IV medication to thin your blood and then get some tests done to confirm my diagnosis. I think you have a blood clot that has traveled from your leg to your lungs, which is why it is hard to breathe. It's called a pulmonary embolism."

She pushed the call bell on the woman's bed and waited for a nurse to join them. "Julie, can you please start a therapeutic intravenous heparin infusion? I am going to order an electrocardiogram and a CT scan of the pulmonary arteries, *stat*."

She touched the woman reassuringly once more and then left to write the necessary orders and contact the on-call radiologist to expedite the tests.

She was staring at the electrocardiogram tracing when a familiar sensation passed over her. She wasn't surprised to see Tate standing beside her. He had changed out of his surgical scrubs and was casually dressed and still devastatingly handsome, with a look of self-possession about him.

"I'm on my way home but I wanted you to have this tonight to celebrate." He passed over a box that was fortunately *not* the same ring box she was all too familiar with. Still she approached it with hesitation, never able to predict Tate's words or actions.

"Open the box, Chloe." He was irritated.

She looked around the department and then did as she was told. Sitting atop the plush velvet was a diamond-encrusted primrose key pendant on a thin platinum chain. It was breathtaking.

"I wanted to give you something to signify our new beginning. Since there is no way I'm going to convince you to put a ring on your finger anytime soon, I thought a key to unlock our future together was a good second choice. The key to the loft is in the box under the velvet."

It was the most romantic thing he had ever said to her and he looked as if he had meant every word. She wanted to kiss him, to reach up and press her lips against his...

"Dr. Darcy to Radiology *stat*. Dr. Darcy to Radiology—*stat*." Their moment was broken and she sent him a desperate look of apology before she took off, running towards Radiology.

"What's going on," she asked on arrival, her eyes drawn to Ms. O'Brien, who appeared non-responsive to the chaos surrounding her.

"She lost consciousness during the scan. We can't get a blood pressure. Her last measured was sixty over twenty-five when we pulled her out of the machine. Pulse is there, but weak and slow," replied the respiratory technician who had been called for help.

"What do we have in here?" she asked looking around the room for basic resuscitation equipment.

"Nothing."

"Then let's move her and run." Chloe grabbed the transfer roller and threw it on the stretcher beside the scan machine. She went around it and rolled Ms. O'Brien toward her, allowing the team to place the board under her and pull her over. Then they were off. "Take her to Trauma One—it's open."

She was winded from her run, her new-found pregnancy limitations still surprising to her.

She looked at the radiology technician, who seemed stunned by the turn in events. "Did you see a clot?"

"The radiologist hasn't reviewed the films yet."

"I understand that, but did you see a clot? It's important," she stressed.

"Yes, I think there is a large saddle embolus between the right and left pulmonary arteries."

"Thank you."

She raced back to Trauma One and saw the team was in action. Ms. O'Brien was wearing a non-rebreather mask and the nurses had established additional intravenous access and hooked her up to the main monitor bank. Her blood pressure was fifty over twenty.

"Give her two liters of intravenous normal saline and establish a norepinephrine infusion on a line separate from her heparin."

"Need help?"

Ryan's voice broke through the crowd and she saw him standing unobtrusively outside the trauma room.

"I'm going to start thrombolytic therapy in addition to her intravenous anticoagulation," she replied knowing she might be out on a ledge.

"Is it worth the risk of a bleed into her head?" he asked, not moving from his spot.

"Yes, she is hypotensive, with a saddle embolus on

imaging and significant right heart strain on electrocardiogram."

"I'll call Pharmacy and have them send up the medication right away."

"Thank you."

She stayed with Ms. O'Brien for hours, well past the end of her shift, until she was stable for transportation to the Intensive Care Unit. Her blood pressure had stabilized and slowly her breathing had improved. She'd regained consciousness and showed no signs of neurological damage from the risky clot-busting medication.

After she'd signed off the chart she changed back into her regular clothes and checked her phone. She had missed calls from Tate, her parents, and Kate. She also noticed the time. It was a minute past twelve. She was officially no longer a resident.

"Congratulations."

The voice cut through her thoughts.

Ryan stood beside her. "I would offer to take you for a drink to celebrate your last shift as a resident, but given your delicate condition and your rather protective baby daddy I think we should take a rain check."

"As long as it's not a permanent rain check. My life is complicated enough these days without having to worry about my friends ditching me."

"Chloe, you know that I haven't been particularly fond of Tate Reed recently, but I think you are doing the right thing. A child does need two parents, and I think you and Tate are both mature enough to work through any differences you have and do what is best to provide that."

"I don't know what to say," she responded, stunned by the change in Ryan's attitude.

"You don't need to say anything. You're doing the right thing and I respect you even more for it."

CHAPTER NINE

TATE ARRIVED JUST as he'd said he would at three o'clock sharp. She finished taping the last of the boxes shut and left it with the others for the movers to put into storage. Tate's fully furnished loft and her changing body meant she had little she needed to bring with her.

"Ready?" he asked as he lingered in the doorway of her apartment.

"Does it matter if I'm not?" she answered. *This was it*.

"No, it doesn't. I'll take you as is."

They both smirked at his confidence and she watched as he took her suitcase from her and they left the apartment. Tate opened the passenger door and helped her into the vehicle before stowing her suitcase in the back. They drove through the winding Boston streets and she took in the beauty of the hot summer day. She barely noticed where they were until the vehicle stopped and her door was being opened for her.

It wasn't Tate's loft. Instead it was one of Boston's finest five-star hotels that overlooked the harbor. She took the cue and left the vehicle, having no idea why she was there but knowing the bellman didn't have the answer. She watched as Tate opened the hatch and pointed out the bags to the bellman before coming around to take her arm.

"Why are we here?" she finally asked as the coolness of the air-conditioned lobby greeted her.

"To celebrate our new beginning." He took her hand, kissing the back of it before leaving her to check in with the hotel's exclusive concierge. Within minutes he was back at her side, leading her to the elevator and then down the hall toward a corner suite.

Before she could move forward he'd reached under her legs and swept her up and into his arms. He carried her in. He didn't put her down as she took in the luxury of the suite, the sitting room and its adjoining balcony, the marble finishes and plush velvet coverings. Then they were in the bedroom, with a king-size bed and a bottle of champagne sitting on ice, followed by the bathroom, where she was finally lowered slowly to her feet. The bathtub was deep and filled with water, bubbles and rose petals.

He gently turned her away from him, his fingers finding the zip of her summer dress and lowering it slowly until the dress was released and fell to the floor. Mesmerized by the moment, she stepped out of it, unabashed in the simple bikini briefs she wore.

"I thought you might like to relax. I know you didn't sleep much last night and it's been a hectic day," Tate explained.

She turned toward him, feeling empowered by his attentions. "Are you joining me?"

He smiled ruefully. "There is nothing I would like more, but if I do it may not be as relaxing and peaceful as intended."

She was disappointed, but appreciative of his intentions.

"Call when you are ready to get out. I don't want you to slip." And after a long, appraising look at her he left.

She felt her body melt into the water. The tub was so

deep that the water sat at her shoulders. She closed her eyes—and awoke to Tate's voice and soft touch.

"Chloe…" He nudged her shoulder gently.

As she adjusted to her surroundings she registered that the water had cooled considerably. "I fell asleep," she confirmed to both of them.

"Yes. Let's get you out before you become a mermaid." She stood with Tate as support, helping her balance. As she stepped out he held a warm towel from the heated towel rack and gently patted the excess water from her before replacing it with an equally warmed robe.

"Thank you," she murmured.

"Do you want to sleep a little longer?" Tate asked.

"I'm good." She looked down at her robe and realized that other than her dress she had nothing to wear. "I don't have any of my things."

Tate smiled. "I packed you an overnight bag and your clothes are in the bedroom. The box on the counter is a present from me." He smiled and left the bathroom.

She walked toward the box, gently pulling at the satin bow and lifting the lid and layers of tissue until she revealed an ivory silk nightgown with thin straps and a deep V front. A rose pattern had been embroidered at the waist, and there was a slit almost to the thigh that allowed for movement and also showed a great amount of leg. She doubted its fit, as her pregnancy now sat midway up her abdomen, but she tried. The material felt cool against her, and it covered her whole body, accentuating the fullness of her breasts and abdomen. She felt sexy, and more confident that she had in a long time.

She emerged from the bathroom in just the nightgown, leaving the robe behind. Tate had stripped from his jacket, and his dress shirt was half buttoned, sleeves rolled up. He was sitting on the large king-sized bed, where the linen had been turned down.

"You look amazing, Chloe."

She smiled at the compliment. "Thank you. So do you—always, really."

"Can I get you a drink?" He gestured toward the champagne bucket.

She smiled and placed her hand on her abdomen. "I don't think that is the best idea, do you?"

"It's sparkling grape juice—for both of us." He opened the bottle and poured two tall flutes of the bubbly liquid. "To new beginnings."

He handed her a glass as she sat down to join him and they clinked them together as he finished his toast. The liquid was cool on her throat. As she lowered the glass she found it taken from her, and the taste of the liquid was quickly replaced by the taste of Tate.

"I've missed this," he murmured against her mouth.

The warmth radiating from him and the lingering scent of his cologne was enough to intoxicate her without any alcohol. "Mmmm..." she murmured in response.

He stopped kissing her and pulled back, his hands cradling her face. "Chloe, do you want me?"

"Yes," she replied unabashedly. "Do you want *me*?" She held her breath, waiting for his response.

His eyebrow rose, and the side of his mouth rose too. He reached for her hand and placed it on his groin, his rigidity pressing through the gray fabric. "Every minute since I last had you."

She could feel his sincerity and took solace in their mutual want. This was where they were equal, and it was not a bad place to be starting from. She met his smile as she reached for his belt. He looked back with desire but didn't stop her. She undid first his belt, then the button, then the fly of his pants, and felt a great sense of pride as the weight and strength of his erection spilled into her hand. She gently brushed her hand against the last layer of fabric between them before turning her attention toward his shirt. She slowly undid every button, allowing her fingertips to brush against the hard musculature. When she reached the final button she pushed the material from his shoulders.

She stood from the bed, holding her hands up to lace her fingers within his, and then pulled him to his feet. She used the change in position to finish her earlier act of removing his trousers, followed by all his remaining undergarments.

"I'm feeling a bit underdressed, Chloe. Are you planning on joining me?" he asked in a sultry voice, showing no embarrassment. Why would he? He was magnificent, and just the sight of his masculine virility was enough to make her throb with desire.

"Yes. Would you like the honor?"

"I would." He pulled her toward him, gathering the soft material into his large hands before raising the entire garment over her head. "Better."

"Make love to me, Tate?" she asked softly, feeling more exposed by her request than her nudity.

He didn't reply with words. Instead he swept her off her feet, laid her on the bed, and complied.

Tate strode into the hospital laboratory ready to fulfill his promise to Chloe. They had spent the past week enjoying and getting to know each other and every day he was happier and more confident in his decision-making. Aside from the luxury of their bedroom compatibility he enjoyed how easy and relaxing she was to be with on the one hand, and how she could challenge and maintain his interest on the other. It was almost everything he had ever wanted.

He still felt Chloe was holding something back from him, and he would bet it had everything to do with the paternity test he was about to have done. She still felt she had something to prove.

He recognized the voice before he saw his face. Ryan Callum was at the desk, speaking with the unit clerk.

"How long does it take for paternity results to come back?" he was asking.

"Two to three weeks, Dr. Callum. We can page you as soon as they arrive."

"Thank you."

Tate was fixed on the conversation and still standing in the doorway when Ryan turned to leave. They met each other's eyes but said nothing as Tate moved aside and let the other man pass.

Why was Ryan Callum getting a paternity test? A glimmer of doubt formed in his mind and started to smolder. He knew better than anyone that sometimes a working relationship could lead to a personal one, and Chloe certainly was a draw that few men could resist. Ryan also had the benefit of knowing her beyond her beauty, which only strengthened her appeal. Had they been more than the friends they were now?

No, it wasn't possible. Chloe would have told him. There was also no way Tate was prepared to consider the possibility that he could lose everything he almost had. But why was Ryan taking a paternity test at the same time as he was?

He walked toward the unit clerk, trying to focus on the task he'd come to perform. "I'm Tate Reed. I believe some requisitions were faxed over from Dr. Erin Madden's office that I need to complete?"

"Yes, Dr. Reed. If you can take a seat for a few minutes we will get the tubes labeled and call for you when we are ready."

He nodded his agreement.

Within fifteen minutes the task was complete, but Tate

had no resolution. He had broken one of the cardinal rules of medicine. He had participated in a test when he had no idea what to do with the results. If there was a possibility he was *not* the father of Chloe's baby did he even want to know? It wouldn't change things. He was committed to Chloe and they were going to raise this child together. But Ryan would know.

The world he had lived in for the past week felt different. It was no longer he and Chloe and the wonder of their new life together and parenthood. It was he, Chloe and Ryan Callum—and he wasn't happy at the new addition to what had briefly been the perfect family.

Chloe rested on the sofa, her feet up and her computer on her lap, as she scanned through the listings Tate's real estate agent had sent over. Tate's loft was perfect for one, sometimes perfect for two, but it was not meant for a family of three.

She felt before she saw the small movement on her abdominal wall as the baby stretched or kicked—or made whatever motion it was fond of doing. She smiled, always happy for a reminder of the wellbeing of her child.

When she looked back at the listings she tried to consider them objectively. Each house was more impressive than the next. At first she had been reluctant. The grandeur and the cost of the homes the realtor had forwarded were beyond her wildest dreams and beyond her budget.

She was already aware that she would be far from an equal financial contributor in their relationship. Tate had arranged for a generous amount of money to be deposited into her personal account to help with her student loans. She had objected, but she hadn't won the fight with Tate, who had argued that he would rather she take care of herself and their baby than work herself past her limits when he easily could afford to take care of all three of them.

The same went for the house. There was no way she could afford even twenty percent of the value of the homes selected, but Tate had once again convinced her that in the long term it would be better to raise their child in a real home, with a real yard, in a good neighborhood, than to move house halfway through their child's childhood, when Chloe finally felt financially equal—which might be never.

General surgeons typically made more money than emergency physicians. And as Tate was one of the top ten vascular surgeons in the country, and had been recruited to Boston General with a heavy incentive package, she had no hope of ever being equal. It was a situation she made herself accept, acknowledging the irony that in all her prior failed relationships the main breaking point had been her boyfriends' inability to accept her advanced education and increased earning potential.

At least the listings were taking her mind off her upcoming ultrasound appointment. After a week of happiness with Tate she had the uncanny feeling that at any moment it was all going to go away. She had spent years pining for Tate and trying to come to terms with the fact that she would never be with him. Now they were together, and with or without love she was happy, and slowly coming to be at peace with their life together. He was considerate, respectful, and definitely attracted to her. Their nightly lovemaking was the only time when her mind managed to shut off and when she truly felt they connected. He was also very interested and attentive to her pregnancy, making sure she was feeling well and taking the time and patience to wait to feel for their baby's movement.

Their baby. She had thought the further she got into the pregnancy the more relaxed she would become, but every day she felt as if she had more and more to lose.

Erin had been very good at explaining the plan for her pregnancy and she felt well cared for, but that didn't mean she didn't worry. Her next ultrasound was one of many, and despite the joy she got from seeing her baby she also remembered the purpose of the scan—which was to look for problems. At least Tate would be there. As independent as she had always been, each day she was more grateful that she wasn't doing this alone.

She heard the key turn and the sound of the loft door opening. Tate walked through and immediately she felt the small flame that always burned for him flare to life. She craved, loved and needed his attention and attraction toward her.

"Hey," she greeted him, smiling at the breathy quality her voice seemed to have adopted around him.

"I went and did the blood work today."

It was a face she recognized but hadn't seen in a while, and she wasn't happy to see it return. Maybe he just didn't like being reminded of the original terms of their union. She already felt past that, and was looking forward to moving on together as a team.

"Thank you. Did they say how long it would take to come back?" She really didn't want to be discussing this further, but she needed to know when or if she would be able to put her mind at ease.

"Two to three weeks," Tate answered, and then he walked through to the kitchen and away from her and the conversation.

He didn't turn back to look at her when he started to talk again, but she could almost see the expression on his face.

"Archer called me a few hours ago. He's had a family emergency and needs me to cover his week of nights."

"Oh." She didn't believe him. Not in light of the distance he was expressing. But she didn't have the strength to confront the truth that he was likely lying to her. She would rather pretend everything was as it should be than risk losing what they had slowly managed to build together.

"I already have an elective day of surgical cases booked for Monday, and a combination of clinics and administrative meetings for the rest of the week, so I won't be around much."

He was giving her notice. Their "honeymoon" was over. What had changed? Was this all about the blood work? Or had he grown tired of her already?

"Is there anyone else that can do it?" She heard the desperation come through in her voice, but desperate was how she felt. She wanted to hold on to what they had.

Tate turned and looked at her, but what he was thinking or feeling she couldn't tell.

"No, Chloe. I owe Archer this favor. He covered for me during your recuperation."

She couldn't argue with that. "What about the ultrasound?" she asked.

"I'll be there."

"Do you want me to reschedule our meeting with the realtor?"

"No, you go. I'm okay with whatever you pick."

"It's our home, Tate, you should be there," she argued.

"I will be, Chloe. But I still have a job to do. My schedule was arranged months ago—before you and the baby."

She could hear his frustration and it was another warning to leave things alone.

"You're starting back again this week too. Between your shift work schedule and my schedule we are going to be lucky to see each other at all. This last week has been great together, but it's not reality—which I think we both need to face."

There was a lot she needed to face, and everything

that had made her think it was going to be smooth sailing from here on evaporated in her mind.

That night was their last together in bed. Tate had been quiet throughout the rest of the evening and she hadn't confronted him again. She had lived in fear that the change in his attitude toward her was going to span all areas, but that night he still reached for her. There was a new intensity and drive toward complete possession that they had never experienced. She cried out his name as he entered her, and with each thrust he begged her to repeat it, until they both tumbled over the edge.

Afterward he said nothing, pulling her against him but facing away.

In the morning he was gone.

CHAPTER TEN

SHE WALKED BACK in to the Emergency Department, aware that everything had changed but feeling no different. She was with Tate, pregnant with his child, and now she was on the attending staff.

"Good afternoon, Dr. Darcy." The unit clerk, whom she had known for the past five years, greeted her.

"Hello, Lexi," she responded, a smile on her face.

She walked to the main triage board and assessed the department. There was a list of who was on shift, both staff and residents, and to which section they were assigned. Next to it was a list of current patients on an electronic mounted flat screen. Names were not listed but demographics were. Location, age, gender, presenting complaint and assigned physician were all listed and updated regularly in order to keep and maintain the flow within the department. People who needed to stay had to be consulted to the appropriate service. Everyone else had to be treated and discharged to make room for the next patient.

She was listed on the board simply as Darcy, and was assigned to Section B: Fast Track. Not the sickest of patients but also not the chronic patients. It was a good place to start on her first day back.

Her first instinct was to grab a chart and begin seeing

patients, but she held herself back. For the first time she was no longer a resident. Her new role was going to be different. She was now responsible for both patient care and the education of the other residents. So instead she waited.

Within five minutes Kristen Inglewood, a third-year in the program, had made her way toward Chloe and she smiled at her good luck. Kristen was excellent, and they had worked well together when they were both residents.

"Hi, Dr. Darcy."

"Hi, Kristen, but as always you can call me Chloe. What have you seen so far?"

"A four-year-old boy presenting with a four-day history of fever, flu-like symptoms and headache."

"Why did they bring him in today?" Chloe asked, knowing there was usually something that had instigated a decision to present to the emergency department.

"New rash that started developing on the cheek yesterday and is slowly spreading toward the torso and limbs," Kristen answered confidently, obviously aware that this was a key part of the history.

"Is he otherwise a healthy child?"

"Yes. In preschool, has been vaccinated according to schedule, and has met all developmental milestones."

"Physical exam?"

"He still appears overall well. He is playing in the room, showing no signs of lethargy. All vitals are within normal limits for his age and temperature is one hundred and one degrees Fahrenheit. Eyes, ears and throat are all normal, with no signs of infection. His chest is clear, with equal respirations bilaterally, and no signs of pneumonia or decreased air entry. The rash is in a lace-like pattern, starting on his left cheek and extending in patches on his torso and left arm."

"Do you have a differential diagnosis?"

"Fifth disease or parvovirus. The other most common condition is adenovirus, but the rash is more typical of Fifth."

"So what do you want to do?"

"Nothing. The child is otherwise well, breathing normally and active. Physical examination is completely within normal limits. I think he's safe to go home with counseling on when to return if he worsens and plans to keep him out of school for the next week."

"Sounds great—let's go see him together."

"Um, Chloe..." For the first time Kristen seemed uncomfortable in their exchange, her eyes focused specifically on Chloe's abdomen.

"Yes, I'm pregnant." She hadn't made any sort of public announcement, but she hadn't had to. In the past two months her pregnancy had become increasingly more visible and now it was undeniable. Coupled with her now public relationship with Tate, she had no doubt there was not a soul in the building who was not aware of the change in her circumstances.

"I know, and congratulations on everything. Dr. Reed is amazing. I was referring to the effects parvovirus has on pregnant women and their babies. If there is the possibility that you are non-immune you should try to avoid direct patient contact."

Chloe knew that—she just had trouble remembering that she was now among that vulnerable group. Pregnant women were at risk for both maternal and fetal complications from many infectious diseases, but she hadn't ever faced any restrictions in what she could and couldn't treat. She also had never had to consider anyone other than herself in the risks she took in her profession.

"Thank you, Kristen. If you're happy and the parents are happy go ahead. I'll sign off on the chart later."

The next few hours were filled with multiple fractures, minor wounds requiring suturing, sore throats, bladder infections and rashes. Between the two of them they kept their section turning over. Chloe, who had already been a conscientious physician, was extra cautious, ensuring she used appropriate contact precautions with any patient who might have an infectious condition.

Now she sat at one of the many physician work stations on the phone, on hold, awaiting a connection with the poison control line. A university student had taken a handful of her roommate's hyperactivity medication in order to help her stay awake to study. Now the young woman was experiencing hallucinations and other psychotic symptoms and Chloe was looking for guidance on other medical side effects they might encounter.

"I brought you something to eat."

Tate's voice entered through the generic music playing on the end of the line. He was standing next to her, also in hospital scrubs, carrying a brown paper bag from the hospital café.

"Thank you." She smiled, still not sure where they were at. "I have a few more things to do, then I will try to take a dinner break."

"You need to eat something, Chloe. You are six hours into your shift and I bet you haven't sat down or eaten anything since you started. I can also bet that you will not do so until at least one to two hours after your shift is done. You need to be conscientious about more than just your job. It is not just you anymore."

"The baby and I are fine, Tate. My work is very important to me, as is the baby, and I am more than capable of taking care of both." She didn't appreciate being told what to do, or any implication that she was making bad choices on their behalf—not even from Tate, who she knew was just being overprotective in light of everything. She worried his new-found protectiveness was more about the baby than her.

"I need help in here!" someone yelled, and broke into their conversation.

Chloe got up and ran to discover her patient's psychotic behavior had escalated and she was physically tearing apart the exam room and attacking one of the nurses.

She went to enter the room, but was held back by a strong grip.

"Not a chance, Chloe."

She watched as Tate entered the room and moved behind the patient, pulling her back and restraining her away from the nurse she had barricaded in a corner.

Chloe yelled down the hall at the other staff who had also come to help. "I need Haldol—five milligrams, IM."

The syringe was in her hands within minutes and she made her way slowly into the room. Tate still held the patient, her back to him, her arms restrained, but she seemed to have calmed.

"Give me the syringe. I don't want her to kick out at you," he said.

It was an order that she followed. Tate's physical strength was enough to hold the patient with one arm as the other injected the medication into the woman's thigh. They both waited and within a few minutes the sedative effect took place.

Now she was sedated, several nurses helped transfer her onto a hospital gurney, where monitors were attached and restraints put in place.

"Thank you," Chloe said as Tate left the room.

"You need to promise me you are going to take better care of yourself. I can't always be here, and I don't like having to spend every moment you are out of my sight worrying about you."

"You mean the baby?" she inferred.

"No, Chloe, I mean *you*." He moved toward her,

pressing his lips hard against her forehead before he walked away.

She stood there speechless for a few moments before she returned to her desk.

She opened the brown bag and did as she was told, eating the granola bar, the fruit cup, and making her way halfway through the bottle of water before she began to chart the incident and call in the consultation to Internal Medicine.

Every time she thought she had Tate figured out he confused her more. It was more than frustrating to someone who had spent her entire career diagnosing and figuring people out.

By the time she had done all her paperwork and handed off her continuing patients her shift had been technically over for two hours. Her stomach growled and the baby kicked out at the disruption. Things had definitely changed. She wouldn't be able to push herself the way she'd used to anymore.

She changed back into her street clothes, lingering to chat, and then slowly made her way home. As she slid open the door she was greeted by her expectation: all the lights were off and Tate wasn't home. She'd known this was likely to be the case, but it still didn't help with her loneliness. For the last five years she had lived alone and never once been bothered by coming home to an empty apartment. But somehow in the last week everything had changed, and now the empty loft was significant for what was missing in her life.

It was three days before she saw Tate again. She was lying on the sonographer's table, her abdomen exposed, when Tate entered the room and took the seat next to her. She looked at him, and he looked tired, with more stubble on his face than normal. She had deliberately avoided confirming his explanation of on call coverage for his absence, and for the first time she had hope that she was wrong. He certainly looked tired enough to have been working double shifts.

"Sorry I'm late," he whispered to her through the darkness of the room.

"It's okay," she reassured him.

As the sonographer began to scan her abdomen images of their baby were transmitted to the screen on the wall in front of them. The first picture was of the baby in profile, the forehead, nose, lips and chin in perfect outline. She felt Tate's hand closing over hers and let go some of the anxiety that had been building within her.

Though they were both medical, it was still hard to interpret all the images they were seeing, but the sonographer explained every structure she was looking at.

"Do you want to know the gender?" the sonographer asked.

Chloe turned to Tate, wanting his input.

"Whatever you want, Chloe."

"It would be nice to wait for a surprise," she said, hoping he felt the same.

"I agree. This baby hasn't been enough of a surprise yet." His beautiful smile and the glint in his eyes were vibrant enough to be seen through the darkness. "No, we don't want to know," he answered for them both.

"Okay, we are just going to start doing a study of the baby's middle cerebral artery. By analyzing how quickly the blood is flowing through the vessel we can predict with some accuracy what the baby's red cell count is."

The sonographer did not say anything else as she worked to capture the baby in the perfect position and then aligned the marker perpendicular to the vessel. She performed the same action over and over again to calculate an average. The first few times Chloe thought nothing of it, but as the sonographer got more quiet and didn't comment on what she was seeing Chloe began to feel her panic start to build.

She turned to Tate, who was alternating between watching the screen and watching her. She felt him squeeze her hand again for reassurance.

"Is there something wrong," he asked directly, after a few more minutes had passed.

"The speed in the blood vessel is high normal. It's not yet abnormal, but it's higher than we would typically see at this stage. I'm going to go and review the images with the perinatologist on call today and she may want to come and re-scan you herself. I'll be right back."

The sonographer used the paper drape that had been tucked into Chloe's lowered pants to wipe the jelly from her abdomen before she left the room.

"The baby looked okay to you, right?" she asked Tate, looking for reassurance, knowing that he didn't know any more than she did.

He used his other hand to stroke through her hair, his hand never leaving hers. "The baby looked beautiful. I would expect nothing less from our child."

The door opened and the sonographer returned, accompanied by a middle-aged woman in a white lab coat. "Dr. Reed, Dr. Darcy, I'm Dr. Young, the perinatologist covering the unit today. Do you mind if I have a quick look at your baby?"

"Go ahead."

Once again warm jelly was applied to her abdomen and the baby reappeared on the screen. Silence filled the room for several more minutes as Dr. Young took a look at the baby and repeated the artery study.

"The studies of the baby's middle cerebral artery are in the high normal range, but not abnormal. The rest of the images look normal, with a normal-sized baby and no evidence of excess fluid around the heart, lungs or amniotic cavity."

"So what's the plan?" Tate asked, before Chloe could voice the same question.

"We are going to arrange weekly ultrasounds to keep a close eye on things. I assume you've both had the appropriate blood work to determine the possible blood types the baby could have?"

"Yes," they answered together.

"Is there anything else we can do? Is Chloe okay to keep working? Should she be at home resting?"

"No, Dr. Reed. This isn't a condition that would benefit from that. Unfortunately there is nothing we can do but keep a close eye on the baby and arrange delivery if the baby starts to decompensate. The antibodies in Dr. Reed's blood have the potential to attack the baby's existing red blood cells if the baby has the associated blood type. The Kell-antibody can also suppress the cells in the bone marrow that produce the baby's red blood cells. If the baby's levels become critically low than we should see an abnormal reading on the test we just performed, or signs of heart failure. At which point it would be safer to delivery prematurely than to leave the baby in its current environment."

"What about Chloe? What are her risks?" Tate asked.

Chloe was still processing the information she had just heard—not that it was new to her, but it was still hard to hear.

"Dr. Darcy is not at any significant risk. In the future it may be harder to find blood products for her, in the event she needs a transfusion, and there is an increased risk of needing a Caesarean birth if we have to urgently deliver the baby prematurely, but overall she is quite safe."

Tate squeezed Chloe's hand again. "Thank you, Dr. Young."

The image on the screen vanished and Chloe felt her abdomen being wiped off once again.

"Dr. Darcy, the receptionist at the front desk has been instructed to rebook you for weekly ultrasounds and blood work so we can follow your antibody levels. She can work with you and Dr. Reed for a regularly scheduled appointment so that you can arrange your schedules around it. Dr. Madden will have your ultrasound report by the end of the day, as well as my recommendations. Have a good day."

They both left the room while Chloe continued to lie on the examination bed. Eventually she felt Tate rearranging her clothing and easing her upright.

"I really need everything to be okay," she confided.

"It will be," Tate answered, more confident than he had any right to be. Still, that was what she needed right now.

They walked from the exam room back to the reception desk and arranged a standing appointment that didn't conflict with Tate's regular operating schedule.

"I need to call my secretary and rearrange a few things—do you mind waiting a few minutes?" he asked.

"No," she answered honestly. She was already adding the weekly appointments to the calendar on her phone, which had been updated to follow her pregnancy. She was twenty-three weeks. A full-grown baby was forty weeks, and she needed to make it until at least twenty-six weeks to have a chance at a healthy newborn.

The pictures hadn't prepared him for seeing the baby today. Watching the sonographer move the probe around Chloe's stomach and watching the matching image on the screen had brought everything home. This was his family.

He had never seen Chloe look more beautiful as she did with her rounded stomach and that expectant glow. But today she had made him catch his breath. He had meant his words to her. The baby *was* beautiful—because he or she already looked like their mother. He had studied the images intently and his mind had filled in the rest. Hope, anticipation, expectancy—no words could describe how much he was looking forward to meeting their child. This baby—*their* baby—felt like the final key to his and Chloe's relationship. The baby was the piece of his life he hadn't known was missing, and it would help him keep the best thing that had ever happened to him— Chloe—forever.

She was still staring at her phone, considering the possibilities when Tate returned.

"Ready to go?" he asked.

"Yes." It wasn't until she was sitting inside his Range Rover that common sense returned. "Tate, don't you have to go back to work?"

"I shuffled the rest of my day and found someone to cover my shift tonight."

"Thank you." She was more than grateful not to be alone with her own thoughts.

"I also called the realtor. She is going to meet us back at the loft and is working now to arrange viewings of the houses you liked. If this baby is going to come earlier than we expected I want us to be settled in to our new home before you deliver. We'll see them today and make a decision together, so you have one less thing to worry about."

"Thank you."

Tate reached over and placed his hand over the one she had resting on her thigh. It was funny, the effect he had on her. His touch brought both a feeling of heat and excitement and also a sense of calm and peace. Everything was going to be okay. She just had to have faith.

When they arrived back at the loft the realtor was in the lobby, waiting for them. The remainder of their day was spent looking at homes, each spectacular in its own right, and a distraction from the news about her pregnancy.

The first was a Victorian-style home that was beautiful, with marble finishes and tall white columns, but it lacked the kind of warmth Chloe could see raising a family in.

The second was more modern, and very similar to Tate's loft. It was a completely open concept, with finishes that were a study of contrasts, alternating boldly between dark and light. It had a large open staircase that transitioned the two floors. It lacked both a railing and a backdrop between steps. It was beautiful for a couple, but she had worked in the emergency department for long enough to know that you would only have to look away for a moment for a child to have a serious accident.

The third house was her favorite from the minute she saw it. It hadn't been included in the listings she had seen previously and must be new on the market. It had a wide porch, with the wide stairs to the entrance flanked by a combination of wood and stone pillars.

Recent renovations were obvious inside, but had been done in keeping with the craftsman-style design. The main floor had been changed to an open concept, with the living room transitioning to a family room divided by a half-wall featuring a two-sided fireplace. The family room was sunk by two steps to define the space. Adjacent to the family room and occupying the entire back wall of the home was a large kitchen that had been renovated to include a double oven, fridge and freezer, and an island that was large enough for a cooktop and preparation sink and still allowed six bar stools to sit opposite as a breakfast counter. The remainder of the floor featured a dining room, an office, a powder room, a guest bedroom with en suite bathroom, and a mud room.

She climbed the stairs, feeling safe and secure with the solid wood railing, wide steps and proper incline. The second-floor landing contained another open concept space, which was being used as a children's play area. She walked to the furthest door and discovered the master bedroom. The room was large enough to easily accommodate a king-sized bed and a sitting area, and also had a two-sided fireplace. She discovered a luxury master bathroom with a soaker tub that had the fireplace as a backdrop, a glass-enclosed shower with multiple shower heads and a ladies' bench, and a double sink. A separate toilet was present within the en suite room, as was an adjoining door to a large master closet that contained "his and hers" everything. She could never imagine having enough clothes to fill half of the space.

She walked slowly through the remaining rooms on the upper floor. Two smaller but by no means small bedrooms were adjoined by a Jack and Jill bathroom. The fourth bedroom was immediately next to the master and had been staged as a nursery. She felt her heart accelerate as she took in the lamb-themed room, complete with soft moss-green walls, a white crib and bedroom set, lamb motifs throughout. An upholstered rocker sat in the corner, and she couldn't resist sitting in it and gliding back and forth. She just needed a few more weeks—just a few—before this could become her reality.

The floor was completed by a third additional full bathroom that was accessible off the main landing.

"Would you like to see outside?" the realtor was asking, and for the first time since she had entered the house she remembered that she was not alone. She looked at Tate, who was smiling at her softly.

"Yes, we do," he answered for them both.

The backyard was a perfect backdrop for the home. The deck extended from the family eat-in kitchen area,

making it an ideal extension for outdoor dining and en-
tertaining. Large leafy trees provided shade and privacy.
The grass around the area was thick and lush, and a children's play set was already there.

"You love it," Tate whispered, his breath warm and
comforting against her ear and neck.

"I really do. Do you?"

"If it means this much to you, then, yes—I do."

He ran the tips of his fingers down her back as he made
his way back toward the realtor, who had given them
some privacy. He returned a few minutes later, leaving the
realtor to wait outside.

"She is going to submit an offer and I have given her
bargaining terms for the remainder of the negotiations.
With any luck we should know by the end of tomorrow
whether it is ours or not."

"Do you really think we are that lucky?" She laughed,
thinking about her hospitalization and the high-risk nature
of her pregnancy.

He rested a hand on her abdomen over the baby while
his lips kissed hers softly, gently parting them with his
tongue for the briefest of tastes and sensations.

"Yes, Chloe, I do."

Tate was at home that night, and despite the earlier news
of the day she felt more relaxed. They ordered in dinner
and relaxed on the patio, with the July heat of the day
still present but now bearable. There was no simmer-
ing tension or cold undercurrents between them. And at
nine that evening the realtor called to confirm that their
offer had been accepted and they could take possession
in two weeks' time.

"That's the August long weekend," Chloe confirmed
aloud, just realizing the significance of the date.

"Yes—is that a problem? Are you working that weekend?"

He was oblivious to the conflict Chloe had detected.

"No, I'm not working. It's the same weekend as Kate and Matt's wedding," she explained carefully, unsure of what reaction she would see.

His face didn't change, but he didn't say anything immediately either. She waited as he seemed to be considering his options. The invitation had arrived a week ago, addressed to both of them, but neither had raised the issue since.

"I'll ask my parents to do the walk-through the day of possession. I don't want you traveling or spending the weekend alone in the Hamptons."

"Are you sure?"

"Yes, I'm sure. Is it okay if we go to bed early tonight? This week of nights has been exhausting, and I still have patients I need to see over the weekend."

"Sure—it's been an exhausting day for me as well."

Tate retreated to the bathroom and she heard the sound of the shower. He hadn't asked her to join him, but this time it didn't surprise her. He needed time alone so she let him be. She moved around the loft, bringing in their glasses from the patio and electronically drawing the blackout blinds. She changed into a light satin chemise and slipped into bed. It wasn't long before Tate joined her, the fresh scent of his soap filling the air. He drew a thin Egyptian cotton sheet over both of them before pulling her to him, aligning her against him in the position they always went to sleep in after they'd been intimate. She could feel his nakedness, but tonight he made no advance, and within minutes his breathing signaled that he was fast asleep.

Tate woke in the night, his heart racing, and with images from his dreams still replaying in his mind. It had been Chloe as she had been on the operating table, bleeding to death, but this time he had been holding a small infant. He'd looked up and seen Ryan Callum in the doorway, waiting for him to hand over the baby, the last part of Chloe he had.

When had he fallen in love with her? He had no idea. It was beyond any logic or explanation that he could think of. He had known a few months after the breakup with Kate that he had never truly been in love with her. But when had he fallen in love with Chloe?

Everything that he ever wanted she had, and he was tortured by the thought of losing her. The *what ifs* made no logical sense to him. He could convince himself that there was no way Ryan and Chloe had been involved. There was no way there was even the slightest possibility that Ryan was the father of his child. But logic had nothing to do with how he felt about Chloe and his fear of loving and losing her played at the back of his mind. He just needed to make it through the next two weeks, when the test results would confirm what he and Chloe already knew. They were a family.

He couldn't lose her—not now, not ever.

He pressed himself against her, needing contact with her to erase the nightmare. She murmured contentedly, her neck arching as her bottom pushed into him. The small satin nightgown she had worn to bed had already risen up to her waist and she was bare against him. He should let her sleep, she'd said she was tired, but he couldn't resist her—he could never resist her.

He pressed his lips to the back of her neck, gently kissed the exposed skin of her shoulder. He captured her swollen breast in his hand, gently kneading the firm globe before turning his attention toward her nipple. The satin slid effortlessly, increasing the sensation. He didn't stop kissing her neck as he trailed his hand down her body, his fingers gentle but insistent as he sampled her core. She was wet and ready for him. Still he tried to remain patient, kissing her as he caressed her back and forth.

She moaned, her breathing escalating into pants and gasps. "Please, Tate," she begged.

That was all he needed to hear. She wanted him.

He elevated her upper leg and slid easily into her from behind. She was tight and contracted against him immediately. His hand returned to its ministrations as he moved in and out of her, rocking them both to the same rhythm as his fingers caressed her. He held himself back, trying to be gentle and waiting for her. It didn't take long before she cried out and arched her back again, the spasms he felt from inside her confirming her climax. He embedded himself deep within her and joined her release.

He stayed where he was, as close to her as possible. She didn't turn or move away from him. Instead he was greeted by the sound of rhythmic breathing that signaled sleep.

"I love you, Chloe," he whispered into her hair before he joined her.

CHAPTER ELEVEN

ALMOST TWO WEEKS and two more ultrasounds later Chloe was starting to feel as if things were actually going to be okay. The readings from the baby's artery hadn't changed and there were no signs of heart failure. She was transitioning into her new role as attending staff and Tate was back to being the man she'd fallen in love with—except now his attention was on her and their baby. She wasn't sure how he was making it happen, but Tate never missed a single appointment or ultrasound.

She was even optimistic about this weekend and Kate's wedding. Maybe it would be the final step Tate needed for closure. Maybe after this he would be able to fall in love again. She could hear it so clearly in her mind—*"I love you Chloe."* She just wanted it to be true.

Tate had arranged to take the day off, so they could get an early start on the four-hour journey that was going to be congested with all the other travelers planning a long weekend at the beach. She looked over at him, wondering if the attraction she felt would ever dissipate. He was stunning, in a tight fitted black T-shirt, blue jeans and aviator sunglasses. His grip on the steering wheel revealed a tan muscled forearm—a tan she knew continued throughout his body.

"How many children do you want?"

His question came from nowhere and she was happy not to be the one driving. There was a high probability that she would have driven off the road in surprise.

"Where did *that* question come from?"

"You're an only child and I'm from a family with four children. I was wondering what you were thinking?"

"I haven't thought about it."

"Did you like being an only child? Would you want just this child?"

"No, I didn't like being an only child. It was lonely—still is. I guess if given the choice I would want this baby to have at least one brother or sister to grow up with and share the family history. Would *you* want to have another baby together?"

"I would have as many children with you as you wanted."

"Don't you think we should wait to see how this one turns out first?" she joked, imagining herself running after a high-spirited toddler.

"I can't think of a better mother for my children."

He reached over and rested a hand on her knee as he kept his eyes focused on the road. She was grateful for the slight distraction. She had no doubt his words were genuine. But she couldn't help remembering a conversation they had had. He had proposed to Kate because he wanted children. Did that mean he had once pictured *Kate* as the perfect mother for his children? If he'd changed his mind about Kate, would he also change his mind about her?

She closed her eyes and tried to block the idea from her mind. She needed to put her trust in Tate. They needed at least a mutual trust between them if there was to be no mutual love.

With ease he pulled in to the inn's main entrance and put the vehicle into "park." The valet opened the door and she barely had time to slip her jeweled sandals back onto her feet. As she stood she smoothed down the fabric of her pink maxi-dress, hoping that it was not as wrinkled as she feared.

"Don't forget this." Tate handed her a straw fedora hat with matching pink ribbon. "I don't want you to burn." He pulled her toward him and kissed her before making his way into the inn's lobby.

"Chloe!" Kate's voice rang out.

They both turned as Kate ran toward them. The two women embraced.

"You look so *beautiful*," Kate gushed.

"Thank you." Chloe gracefully accepted the compliment. She rested her hands on her baby bump, proud at the progress and the changes that had happened since Kate had moved back to New York a month ago.

"It's nice to see you too," Tate teased Kate, standing slightly back from the best friends' reunion.

"Hi, Tate." Kate reached up for a brief hug. "Thank you for being the man who brought my best friend to my wedding." She teased him right back.

Chloe laughed and looked up to share her smile with Tate. So far everything felt easy, with no tension between them, and she was grateful.

"Tate."

"Matt."

Both women paused in their conversation as the men in their lives shook hands.

"Chloe, you do look wonderful," Matt greeted her, and she hugged him. She liked Matt. He made Kate happier than she had ever known her to be.

"Thank you—and congratulations to you both."

"I'm going to get us checked in." Tate left the group and made his way to the inn's front desk.

"So what's the plan?" Chloe asked. She would do anything she needed to make sure her best friend had the perfect wedding day.

"I thought you would want to rest when you got here. Tate said you still get quite tired and would likely need an afternoon nap."

"When did you talk to Tate?" Chloe asked, surprised by the knowledge that the two were still speaking often.

"When I called to check on you I wanted the whole truth, and not the stoical version you like to report," Kate replied honestly.

Her friend didn't look angry, and Chloe knew she didn't have a leg to stand on. Hadn't she spent the last six months trying to pretend she was okay to Kate when she wasn't?

"Later on this afternoon you and I have appointments at the inn's spa for manicures and pedicures, and then we have a small rehearsal dinner with you two, Matt's best man and his wife and our families." Kate's excitement was apparent.

"I think the nap was a good thought," Chloe remarked happily, sharing Kate's enthusiasm.

"Yes, well, I need you to take very good care of the little person inside you. His or her mommy is my best friend."

"Thank you, Kate."

"We are all set," Tate informed her as he re-joined them. "Kate, you'll have more than enough time with Chloe later this afternoon."

"Yes, Dr. Reed," Kate quipped, her smile never fading.

Tate led Chloe to the elevator bank and up to their room. It was a corner suite, with a wraparound balcony that opened itself up to an ocean view. Facing the window, a king-sized bed adorned in white linen was centered on the opposite wall. Nautical accents were throughout, and the adjoining bathroom was equally grand, with a two-person whirlpool bathtub and a large shower. The valet had already deposited their luggage prior to their arrival, and sounds from the ocean filled the room.

"It's beautiful," Chloe remarked, venturing out onto the balcony to take in the fresh scent of the ocean.

"It's not the only thing that is," Tate murmured. His arms were braced on either side of the railing and his lips were against the back of her neck.

"I thought I needed my afternoon nap?" she teased, knowing there was no way she would ever be able to refuse him.

"Maybe I need to have an afternoon nap with you."

The rest of the day was filled with equal pleasure and pampering. At the spa, she and Kate gossiped like the old times—about work, their families, and now for the first time about the men in their lives. Chloe didn't speak much about her relationship with Tate, not wanting Kate to draw comparisons with what they had shared, but the bride-to-be was exuberant enough in her love of Matt that Chloe wasn't sure she could have gotten a word in anyway.

Manicures were a rare treat for Kate, who couldn't wear nail polish in the operating room, and they both enjoyed being able to take the time out for indulgence.

Chloe was worried about re-introductions at the rehearsal dinner. The last time Kate's father and stepmother had seen Tate he had been their daughter's boyfriend. Now he was with her visibly pregnant best friend, and she wasn't sure how they would react.

As is turned out, they didn't. They welcomed Tate like an old friend and fussed over Chloe, whom they had both known for the past nine years, smiling the same smile that everyone else did at Kate and Matt's happiness. The entire evening relaxed into one of celebration, ending around eleven so the bride could get her beauty sleep—not that she needed it.

"Are you ready?" Kate asked, her eyes still bright and showing no sign of fatigue.

"Yes, I will be the best maid of honor anyone has ever seen."

"Then let's go." Kate smiled, pulling Chloe to her feet.

"Where are we going?" Chloe looked between Tate and Kate. Both were smiling back at her.

"Well, it's the night before my wedding and I am not going to spend it alone. Your lovely Tate has been kind enough to loan you out for the evening."

She looked back at Tate, who looked more than pleased at his surprise.

"He's a very generous man," Chloe agreed. She was pleased with Kate's openly referral to Tate as Chloe's.

She and Kate left the private dining room, giggling like the schoolgirls that they truthfully had never been. After their first meeting in medical school this felt like the only time they had ever had together when there was no stress over the next exam, or the next milestone in their careers they had to achieve before them. It was a feeling of elation that Chloe couldn't explain.

Kate's room was the honeymoon suite—the top floor of the inn, with panoramic views and the same luxuries Chloe had seen in her own room. Kate had bought them matching pyjamas and they both changed, took off their make-up and crawled into the king-sized bed. *This is what it would have been like to have a sister,* Chloe thought.

The lights from the outside boardwalk filled the room. With the windows open a fresh breeze lifted the summer heat.

"Can you believe we are here?" Kate asked, her voice piercing the darkness.

"Honestly? No."

"I don't think I would have believed anyone if this time last year they'd told me all this was possible."

"All of this?" Chloe asked.

"Reuniting with Matt. Finally hearing and knowing that he loves me back after all the heartbreak and time that had passed between us."

"Was it worth it?" Chloe asked, feeling as if all her future happiness was riding on Kate's answer.

"Was what worth it?"

"The waiting? The pain of loving someone who doesn't love you back?"

"Yes. I would have never said that at the time, but definitely yes. Once I fell in love with Matt I knew that I would never love any other man the same way and as much as I did him. I hated him for years, thinking that he'd ruined any chance of happiness for me, but now I'm actually grateful. My love for Matt was what kept me from settling for anything less and making bad decisions that would have affected more than just *my* life."

"You mean Tate?" Chloe acknowledged painfully.

The bed shifted as Kate turned on her side to look at her and meet her eyes.

"Chloe, I love Tate. But I was never *in* love with Tate. The thing that has brought me the most happiness this year—other than being in love and reunited with Matt—is you and Tate. I meant what I said when I found out you were together. It makes sense."

"He wanted to marry *you* first."

"Yes, he proposed to me, but there was a lot more wrong with our relationship than just my feelings for Matt. We both can see that now. I made logical sense to Tate; you drive him crazy. Sometimes fate can be our best friend."

"Is this Dr. Kate Spence, General Surgeon, talking?" Chloe joked, attempting to lighten the seriousness of their conversation and lessen the risk that she might pour her heart out to Kate and ruin the night before her wedding with her own insecurities and problems.

"No, this is soon-to-be Mrs. Matthew McKayne and her best friend, I suspect the soon-to-be Mrs. Tate Reed, talking."

"You are not really changing your name, are you?" Chloe joked with a playful nudge.

"Never—we've both worked too hard to become Drs. Spence and Darcy!"

Everything went as planned, and Chloe glowed as she walked down the aisle ahead of Kate. A spaghetti-strapped royal-blue silk dress hung from her shoulders. Two triangles of fabric covered her chest and transitioned to an empire waist, which accentuated her new figure and flowed to the floor softly. Kate was stunning in a white silk gown that had been sculpted in waves and tucks that hugged her figure and was mermaid-like in its design.

The ceremony was beautiful, timed perfectly for sunset, and Chloe cried with happiness through it all. Kate was the most beautiful and the most happy Chloe had ever seen her, and she felt no sense of jealousy, only happiness for her friend. There was so much that was positive about the day that there was no room for any negative thoughts or feelings.

Later she watched as Kate and Matt danced together on the lantern-lit patio and she swayed along to the music from the band.

"How are my two favorite people?" Tate asked, holding a glass of wine for himself and a sparkling water for her. He was stunning in his black suit, complete with a navy tie that accented her dress.

"We're wonderful. Do you realize that our baby is now

exactly twenty-six weeks? Every day we get from here on is a blessing."

"And here I thought every day you were with *me* was a blessing."

"You know what I mean."

"Can we interrupt and ask for a dance?"

Kate's voice broke through their exchange. Chloe looked up to see the happy couple before them.

"I think we can manage that." Tate stood from his chair and took Kate's hand, leading her on to the dance floor.

It took Chloe a moment before she realized the invitation also included her, and she too rose, a little wobbly on her silver heels, her focus not entirely on her long silk dress that barely cleared the floor. Before she could right her own balance Tate was behind her, his hands along her back and on her elbow.

"I'm okay," she reassured him, embarrassed by the commotion.

Kate, the bride, was standing abandoned in the center of the dance floor, and Chloe had no idea how Tate had even seen her, never mind managed to get back to her after her small lack of balance.

He didn't seem to believe her as he knelt in front of her, tightening the ankle straps on her silver heels.

"Tate, I'm okay—really."

"Be careful with her, Matt. There is no one else like her."

Matt responded with a small affirming nod and Tate walked away reluctantly back toward Kate.

Matt took her arm and walked her to the dance floor, away from Kate and Tate, before placing his hand on her side and holding her. They started moving to the slow waltz. She couldn't take her eyes off Tate dancing with Kate in her wedding dress, and even though there appeared to be nothing romantic between them it still unnerved her.

"You need to let it go, Chloe."

She turned her head to face Matt.

"Excuse me?" she asked, not sure she had heard him correctly.

"The past. There is nothing we can do to change the past, and thinking about it only punishes them and tortures us. It's not fair to anyone."

She was stunned, and worried that her emotions had always been this transparent. "How can you forget it?" she asked, thinking that Matt was probably the one person who most closely understood her situation.

"I haven't. But I also know that in my situation the only one I have to blame is myself. I made the wrong choice and it cost me nine years with the woman I love."

"I'm not who he wanted. Tate chose Kate over me, Matt."

"Did he really? I wasn't around then, but I'm not sure it was a fair competition. And even if he did, people make mistakes, Chloe. Are you really going to punish him for the rest of your lives together?"

"I'm not punishing him. We're together and having a child," she tried to argue, but as his words sank in she knew he was right. She was punishing both of them and it wasn't making her happy.

"Chloe, a few months ago you did me the biggest favor of my life by telling me that Kate had followed me to New York. Let me do the same for you. Tate loves you. Fortunately for me—and him—he doesn't look at my wife the same way he looks at you."

With perfect timing she looked up and saw Tate looking over Kate's shoulder directly at her. Saw the small upturn at the corner of his mouth and the same piercing green eyes she missed when he was not around.

The music stopped and Matt led her off the dance floor back to her chair. "Get over the past, Chloe, and you'll see that I'm right about the present."

They arrived back in Boston late Monday evening. The rest of the weekend had been relaxing and restful. Chloe missed Kate, and knew the next twenty-three months would be torture. How had she ever thought they needed time apart? The only person uncomfortable with their current situation appeared to be *her*. She thought of Matt's words, appreciating his advice and willing him to be right.

Once back in Boston they went directly to see their new home. Tate turned on the entry light and a warm glow reflected off the polished wood surfaces. The house was empty of all of its furnishings, but full of possibilities in her mind.

"I've arranged for the movers to come to the loft tomorrow while we are at work and move the basics so that we can start living here. The rest of the furnishings you can take your time and choose yourself. Or hire a designer to do it—whatever you would prefer and will cause you the least amount of stress."

"Thank you." She still couldn't believe the home was theirs, awaiting the completion of their family. She rubbed her hand over her stomach and was rewarded by the small flip-flop from inside.

"I thought you would appreciate this one design choice, though," he said, and took her hand and led her upstairs.

She thought he was going to bring her to the bedroom for a romantic surprise; instead they went through the door beside it.

It was the nursery, with all the furnishings she had seen in it before and more. In addition to the furniture and gentle lamb theme the nursery was now stocked and complete. A change table held the smallest diapers she had ever seen, and baby wipes, blankets, lotions and creams. On the dresser was a framed ultrasound photo of the baby's profile, with the caption "Love at First Sight." She opened the top drawer of the dresser to find neatly folded rows of green and yellow baby clothes. The bookshelf was piled with books for children aged from zero to five years.

"How did you do all this?" she asked incredulously. She didn't even know what half the stuff in the nursery was for.

"It was easier than I thought it would be. My sisters made me a list of must-haves for a new baby and after one trip to the baby store I think I bought double. I want everything to be ready and perfect for our baby."

"Thank you. I love it. And please thank your sisters."

"You can thank them yourself next time we see them."

"I like your family." She smiled, enjoying again the feeling of being a part of something she'd never had.

"That's good, because my family includes the both of you."

She smiled again. Matt's words echoed in her head. Was there a possibility that Tate loved her back? Did she have the courage to ask and risk the answer breaking her heart?

CHAPTER TWELVE

TATE WALKED THROUGH the Emergency Department, his eyes searching for Chloe. He had nothing he needed to tell her, but after spending four straight days together at Kate's wedding it was hard to be apart. They had arranged for him to pick her up later that evening, so they could go to the house together for their first night in their new home, but he didn't want to wait that long to see her. Tonight was the night he was going to lay it all on the line and tell her he loved her.

He walked into Section B and up to the attending physician desk. She wasn't there, but Ryan Callum was, with his back turned to him, a phone pressed to his ear. Tate had turned to leave, having no desire to talk to the other man, when Ryan's words caught his attention.

"So the child is mine."

A knife cut through Tate's chest and he had to think how to breathe again.

"Has Dr. Madden been made aware of the results? Thank you for letting me know right away. I appreciate your discretion in this matter."

Tate felt his world come crashing down. It reminded him of seeing Chloe in critical condition on the operating room table. Ryan was the baby's father. He was going to lose the woman he loved and the family he'd always wanted.

Ryan turned, and there was no avoiding a confrontation with the other man.

"What are your plans?" Tate asked, already needing to know how much time he had left. Could he still win her heart?

"Excuse me?" Ryan seemed taken aback by the question, which irritated Tate even more.

"What are you planning to do about the baby?" *My baby*. It still so very much felt like his baby.

"I don't think that is any of your business."

"Answer the question, Ryan." His need to know was paramount.

"I'm going to be the father my child deserves."

"What about her?" He couldn't even say Chloe's name. Not to Ryan.

"That's between us, Tate. Now, if you'll excuse me, I'm done talking about this."

Ryan walked away from Tate and with defeat coursing through him he let him.

Chloe walked toward Tate's office her nerves already on edge after Erin's phone call. The blood work had come back. Both she and Tate carried one copy of the dominant Kell blood-type gene, meaning the baby had a seventy-five percent chance of being affected by the antibody. The only good news was that Tate carried one copy of the C blood-type gene, so there was only a twenty-five percent chance of effect. It would have been much better the other way around, with the Kell gene being more harmful, but it was something they were going to have to live with. Erin had moved up her next ultrasound to tomorrow, and she had already been to the lab to have more blood drawn for an evaluation of her current antibody levels.

Tate's door was shut, so she knocked, thinking that

something serious must have happened to keep him from picking her up and going to their new home together as planned.

"Come in," his voice directed.

She walked in, surprised to find him in the office despite the vocal confirmation she had just heard. She'd anticipated that he would be dealing with a surgical emergency, not sitting at his desk sipping from a glass of Scotch.

She shut the door behind her and took a seat in one of the tall leather-backed chairs across from his desk.

"You didn't meet me as planned," she commented, still trying to take in the picture of the man in front of her. His eyes were bloodshot, his short hair somehow askew, and he hadn't changed from the surgical scrubs he had operated in that day. The only time she had ever seen Tate look like this had been after his breakup with Kate.

"The blood work came back." His voice was a monotone.

This was not the Tate she was used to. Throughout everything he had been the positive one, the reassuring one, and she had expected, had *needed* that trend to continue.

"It's not that bad, Tate." She flipped from her need to be reassured to being reassuring. One of them needed to hold things together. She could do that.

"Isn't it?" A single eyebrow was raised as he looked at her questioningly.

"It's nothing we can't get through." She reached her hand across the table, waiting for him to take it; he didn't.

"The results don't change how you think of me, Chloe? How you feel about our family?"

She could see and feel the hurt coming from him. She'd had no idea he would feel so responsible for something they had no control over.

"No, Tate, they don't. We can get through this to-gether."

He looked as if he didn't believe her. He certainly made no attempt to provide her with the same comfort.

"What about Ryan?" The words were apparently ripped from him out of the amount of pain he appeared to be in.

"What *about* Ryan?" she echoed back, completely lost as to what the question actually meant.

"What's going to happen?" Tate clarified, as though he was making perfect sense—which he was not.

"How would I know? How would *Ryan* even know? High-risk obstetrics and antibody complications in preg-nancy are not really something the average emergency room physician knows anything about."

"He hasn't contacted you since finding out?" Tate sneered, his disdain for Ryan more apparent than ever.

The uneasy feeling that had filled her since Tate had failed to meet her as planned grew to tsunami-sized pro-portions within her.

"Found out *what*, Tate? Spell it out." Her compassion was leaving her and she braced herself for what was com-ing next.

"That Ryan is the baby's father."

For the first time since her hospitalization she felt her full temper and sense of fight return to her. She stood from her chair, her body hanging over his desk, her face as close to his as her pregnant abdomen and the depth of his desk would allow, so she could look him in the eye as near as possible.

"The only person I know to be the father of my child is *you*, Tate."

"I went to the department earlier this evening to see you. I heard Ryan on the phone. The paternity test con-firmed him as the father."

He wasn't angry, despite her escalation, but that still

didn't derail her temper. She collapsed back into her chair, anger seething from every pore.

"*What* paternity test, Tate?"

"The one you asked me to complete."

"Do you mean the blood work I asked you to complete?"

"Yes."

"You thought that was a *paternity* test?"

"Wasn't it?"

She saw the glimmer of doubt begin to cross his mind, but she didn't care.

"You thought I didn't know who the father of my baby was? You thought that I was sleeping with my attending staff? *Ryan?* And you actually thought I would be with you with all those things in mind? Wow, Tate. You really do think highly of me."

Tears of anger and hurt spilled from her eyes, but she didn't care. Nothing could be more humiliating than being faced with the truth about the way Tate really saw her. She had been wrong, thinking he saw past her beauty and saw her for who she truly was. She stood and headed toward the door, away from the man she loved.

She felt him reach for her arm but she pulled it away, not wanting anything physical between them.

"I heard Ryan on the phone today, Chloe. He said the child was his."

"Let me say this once and I am never, *ever* going to say it again. I have never had any type of romantic or sexual relationship with Ryan Callum or any other physician, or any other person that works at this hospital, other than you. The fact that I have to even *say* this to you now is degrading, and I do not deserve it. In the past two years I have slept with exactly one man—you. So, whether you chose to believe it or not, this is *your* baby."

"The blood work—"

"The blood work was *not* a paternity test. It was a genetic work-up for both you and I to determine all the possible combinations of blood types our baby could have beyond the routine A, B and O statuses that come up on basic screening. *That* is what came back today. The baby has a seventy-five percent chance of being affected by severe anemia, which I really thought would be the worst thing I'd hear today. I was wrong."

"Chloe—" He reached for her again.

"No, Tate, I can't. Not anymore—not knowing how you really feel."

She left the office and he didn't follow her. She didn't want him to. It hurt too badly right now, and she didn't need any more revelations from Tate to add to the grief within her.

She had changed and retrieved her purse from the women's locker room before going looking for Tate, so now she had no idea where to go.

The loft had no furniture left in it and she couldn't go to their new house—not alone, and not like this. That house represented everything she had almost had. She dug her phone from her purse and dialed before thinking.

"Hello?" Kate's voice answered.

"Hey, I'm sorry to interrupt your honeymoon, but I need you."

"Chloe?" Kate's voice was questioning, and she knew that she didn't sound like her normal smile-through-the-pain self.

"Yes, it's me."

"Chloe, what's wrong? What's happened?"

"Tate thought the baby was Ryan's."

"Chloe…"

Kate's voice did not contain the surprise and outrage she had expected.

"Kate, he actually thought there was the possibility I was sleeping with my staff and didn't know who the father of my baby was," she explained, waiting for the response she needed from her friend.

"Chloe, I need to be honest with you. Before I learned about you and Tate I thought Ryan was the father too."

"What? How?"

This wasn't helping. It was supposed to be helping.

"Chloe, I didn't know you had anyone in your life, never mind Tate. Ryan Callum is amazing, and quite frankly the idea of pursuing a romantic relationship with your staff is not that foreign to me. After the ectopic he seemed very protective of you, and you were secretive about the paternity. I put two and two together and got the wrong answer."

"I can't believe that the two people I love most in the world both thought the worst of me."

"No, Chloe. I did not assume that you were sleeping with Ryan to get ahead with your career. I know you are more sensitive about those rumors than you pretend to be, and that wasn't what I was thinking. I thought you were in private relationship with a man who happened to be in your department and at the time was your superior. Just like Tate and I had been."

"No, Kate. *Nothing* is like you and Tate had been. And apparently it never will be. I need to go. I'm sorry for dumping all this on you. I'll be okay. I just need some time."

"Chloe…"

"Really, it's okay, Kate. Everything's forgiven. I mean, how was I to expect you to know that I was in love and sleeping with your ex-boyfriend?"

"Chloe…"

"I really have to go. I'll be okay. I'll have to be."

"Take care of yourself, Chloe—please."

"I will. Love you."

CHAPTER THIRTEEN

SHE SPENT THE night in a hotel and arrived at the hospital with enough time to change into the spare clothing she kept in her locker. Her ultrasound had been arranged for eight in the morning, as an emergency spot. She needed the reassurance of seeing her baby. She hadn't had time to tell Tate about the scan—not amidst his confession that he believed Ryan Callum had fathered her pregnancy.

Used to the routine, Chloe shifted down her pants and moved toward the right-hand side of the table within the sonographer's reach. The images were transmitted to the screen and she watched her baby. The sonographer said little as she began taking measurements. First she started to measure the fluid around the baby, and even to Chloe's eyes it seemed to have grown substantially, with the black of the fluid now overwhelming the screen. Then she started scanning the baby, her silence making Chloe look again at what she was seeing on the screen.

She had had enough ultrasounds in her pregnancy to know what things should look like, and they didn't look the same. She had also done several ultrasound courses as a part of her emergency training, so she easily recognized the fluid collections that had started in the baby's lungs, heart and abdomen.

"I'm going to call Dr. Madden and the perinatologist," the sonographer declared, before leaving the room.

There were no false reassurances provided. The baby was in heart failure; Chloe didn't need anyone to tell her that.

Erin walked through the door, her face full of concern, obviously breathless. "Chloe, when did you last have anything to eat or drink?"

She knew the intention behind the question and swallowed hard. "Last evening," she answered. "The baby's in heart failure." She stated her worst fear.

"Yes," Erin confirmed. "I'm sorry, Chloe, but we need to get you delivered."

"I'm not ready," she said, panicked. "The baby's not ready. I'm only twenty-six and a half weeks," she explained, knowing she didn't need to remind Erin of this fact, but not having the strength to ask what she really meant.

"There is no other option, Chloe. The heart failure and the reverse blood flow in the umbilical cord shows that the baby is at high risk for stillbirth at any moment. Dr. Young is reviewing the images and she is on phone to the Neonatal Intensive Care Unit now, letting them know what to expect with the baby."

"Erin, what's going to happen?" she asked, preparing herself for the worst, her mind racing with a thousand horrible thoughts a minute.

For the first time since entering the room Erin slowed herself and took the seat next to Chloe that Tate normally sat in.

"Right now the baby weighs about two and a half pounds, but some of that is swelling from the extra fluid that has built up in the baby's tissues. Following birth the baby will be intubated for respiratory support, and also given some medication down a tube and into its lungs to help the lungs mature and make breathing easier. We can use the umbilical cord to establish intravenous and arterial access so that we can both monitor the baby and provide medication and nutrition in a more direct fashion. There is at least an eighty percent chance of survival and a fifty percent chance of no major complications."

"I haven't exactly been doing great in the luck department this year, Erin."

"Chloe, we need to focus on the positive. We diagnosed the baby before anything really horrible happened and we are going to get you delivered right away."

"A Caesarean section?" she questioned.

"Yes. It's the fastest way, and the baby is still breech right now, making a vaginal delivery a poor option."

"Okay." She nodded, processing the information and agreeing to the plan simultaneously. She needed to be strong for both of them.

"They are preparing the obstetrics operating room across from the nursery. We need to walk to the unit now and get you admitted so we can deliver this baby as soon as possible."

"Okay," she said again, taking everything step by step.

Erin reached over and grabbed the paper drape that was still tucked in, wiping the jelly from her body. She offered Chloe an arm and eased her from the bed. She grabbed her bag and walked with her quickly, but as calmly as possible.

"Chloe, when you get on the unit it is going to be chaotic. Everyone is going to be coming at you, asking you questions, getting you changed, poking and prodding you to get you ready. I have to make a call and get changed into my scrubs. Just remember that you and this baby are going to be okay. Do you have any questions about the plan or the Caesarean?"

"No."

"Chloe, do you want me to call Tate?"

"Yes." She was keeping it together on the outside, but on the inside she was absolutely terrified. Tate needed to be here. It was his baby and he needed to make sure it was okay. She rubbed her stomach again, trying to transmit a sense of reassurance to the person inside her that they were both going to be okay.

True to Erin's word, the scene inside the unit was one of organized chaos. It reminded her of the Emergency Department, except this time she was at the center of the chaos and not directing the team.

She wasn't sure how much time passed before she was sitting upright on the operating table, her legs dangling in front of her, crouched over a pillow, while the anesthetist cleaned her back. She worked hard to focus on staying calm, repeating to herself and her unborn child, *It's going to be okay*, silently in her head. She barely noticed the cold antiseptic on her back, or the sting of the freezing needle. Within minutes her legs and bottom felt warm, and nurses were lifting her legs and lying her on the table.

She watched as things continued to move quickly around her. With the spinal anesthetic she once again felt like an outside observer, able to see but not to feel the cleaning solution on her belly or the drapes being applied.

She looked around at the room, which had no fewer than ten people in it. In the corner was a neonatal resuscitation bed, surrounded by the staff neonatologist, two nurses and a respiratory technician. Around her there were three nurses that she could count, Erin, and an obstetrics resident she didn't know well, but who was there to assist. The anesthetist at the head of the bed shifted the bed for a left tilt and threaded oxygen prongs into her nose.

"Is Tate coming?" she asked, realizing they were moments away from the birth of her baby. She couldn't do this alone.

The operating room door was pushed open and familiar green eyes locked with hers. The rest of him was covered in a surgical mask, hat and scrubs.

"Dr. Reed, you can take this stool beside your wife," the anesthetist instructed.

He did as he was told, not bothering to correct the anesthetist's terminology. "I'm so sorry, Chloe," he whispered, his hands gently stroking her forehead.

"I'm scared," she confessed in a whisper, only to him.

"Chloe, can you feel anything?" Erin asked, her head and scrub hat visible at the top of the extended drape.

"No." Were they touching her?

"Patient is Chloe Darcy. She is having an emergency Caesarean section. She has no allergies. There are two units of blood in the room, and she received a gram of Ancef at nine-thirty-two. Does anyone have any concerns?" the circulating nurse asked as she completed the pre-surgical safety pause.

"No," Erin answered.

"You can proceed," the anesthetist confirmed.

The room, which had been loud and busy in the build-up to this moment, was silenced. Chloe heard Erin call for instruments and the sound of the cautery and suction machines intermittently turning on and off. She glanced over to the resuscitation bed, knowing that in a few minutes her baby would be there. The entire neonatal team was fixated on her abdomen.

"Are you okay?" Tate whispered, his eyes watching her for a response to the surgery.

"I can't feel much—just some tugging and pressure," she replied, trying to focus on the physical and not on the avalanche of chaos her emotions were.

"Uterine incision," she heard a nurse call out to the team.

"Chloe, you are going to feel some pressure on your

abdomen as we help push the baby out. Tate, if you want to stand up you can watch your baby being born. The baby is breech, so you are going to see legs and bum first," Erin described.

Tate looked at her.

"Go ahead," she encouraged.

She watched Tate as he watched. She heard the sound of amniotic fluid splashing the drapes and the floor and felt increased pressure as they pushed at the baby from above. Tate's face stayed set in a look of disbelief and didn't change until a small whimper broke through the silence.

She watched as the resident assistant walked the baby over to the neonatal team, but before she could catch a glimpse the baby was surrounded.

Tate sat down next to her, his hand clutching hers, which was strapped to an arm board.

"He's small, but he's okay."

She wasn't sure which one of them he was trying to reassure.

"It's a boy?" she asked.

"Yes, Chloe. We have a son."

Never had she seen any man look so proud.

"Tate, I think I'm going to be sick."

His smile quickly vanished as he turned his attention toward the anesthetist and they worked together to roll her head to the side.

She was aware of the blood pressure cuff squeezing her arm and of the noise in the room, which appeared to be increasing.

Erin was calling for the blood to be opened and for medication and equipment she had never heard of. She didn't feel well...everything was blurry. She looked again for the baby. One of the nurses had moved and she could see the outline of his little body. His face was covered by a mask as the respiratory technician provided respiratory support.

Tate stood again from his stool and looked over the drape. This time all the blood drained from his face.

A neonatal nurse came around the bed to speak with Tate. "Dr. Reed, we are going to be transporting your son across the hall to the Neonatal Intensive Care Unit. Would you like to come with us?"

"Go," Chloe urged through the oxygen mask that moments ago had replaced the nasal prongs.

"No," Tate refused.

"Please, Tate. I don't want him to be scared and alone."

"He's in excellent hands, right?" Tate questioned the nurse.

"Yes, Dr. Darcy. We will take very good care of your son."

Tate clutched her hand strongly. He felt so warm compared to her. "You should go and be with your son," she tried to argue, but all she wanted to do was sleep.

He bent his head toward her and pushed back her hair and the surgical hat that was attempting to cover it. "Chloe, the most important person in the world to me is right here, and nothing could make me leave you right now. I didn't care if the baby wasn't mine—I was just terrified you would leave me if he wasn't. All I want is you. I love you, and I am going to spend the rest of our lives together reminding you of that every day until you believe me."

"We need another four units of packed cells and two of fresh frozen plasma crossed and in the room. Open the postpartum hemorrhage tray and have a hysterectomy tray standing by, please," Erin commanded.

"It's going to take at least an hour to cross her for more blood," the anesthetist responded.

"Then let's get on it," Erin responded, and even Chloe could hear her friend's fear.

Darkness was descending on her. It reminded her of being on the locker room floor and she was terrified. "Tate!" she cried out.

"Chloe, I'm here, and you are going to be okay. I promise you."

"I love you," she whispered, before she lost the battle and slipped into the darkness.

She opened her eyes to familiar surroundings. She was on the postpartum unit. She tried to move but felt a familiar pain in her abdomen. A hand brushed her forehead and she took comfort and settled with the touch.

"You're okay, Chloe. Rest."

She closed her eyes again and was unsure how much time passed before she reopened them. Tate was sitting at her bedside, still in hospital scrubs, his attention entirely fixated on her. Her hand moved to her abdomen, which was flat. A new wave of panic passed through her.

"He's okay. He has been stabilized and is settling into the nursery, Chloe. Erin was able to stop your bleeding with a special suturing technique and she didn't need to resort to a hysterectomy. We have a beautiful son, Chloe."

"A little boy..." she affirmed, remembering the brief glimpse she had seen.

Tate took her hand and she felt his warmth transmitted through her.

"I love you, Chloe Darcy."

Her eyes swelled and she felt the tears start to roll down her face. She felt completely not in control of anything—including her emotions.

"Because of our son?" she asked. Her fear that he was with her because of the baby was still ever present.

"No, Chloe. But I will forever be grateful to him for helping me keep you."

"Because you can't have Kate?"

She watched his reaction as closely as she could through the haze of pain and the medication she had been given. She needed to be clear. She needed complete honesty and openness. She had been through too much to expect any less.

"I'm your second choice, Tate." She confessed the painful thought that had tortured her for months.

"No, Chloe, you are my first choice. You saved me from myself. I made a horrible mistake in my relationship with Kate. I thought because she met the criteria of what I wanted in a woman that was enough. It wasn't until I met you that I realized what I really needed. I *need* you, Chloe. I need my confident, caring, beautiful partner—even if you drive me absolutely crazy sometimes."

"You avoided me. You never told me how you felt." She loved every word he was saying, but still it didn't make sense to her.

"I was scared of you and of the way you made me feel. At first I didn't trust myself to make a commitment ever again, and I thought an affair would hurt you so I tried to stay away. When I couldn't I became even more terrified that if I admitted to myself I loved you it would break me to lose you—and it would, Chloe. I don't want my life without you."

"I don't want to be without you either, Tate."

For the second time in their relationship Tate lifted her from her hospital bed and held her. His lips kissed hers before she was tucked carefully into his warm embrace and she once again let her tears flow—but this time tears of happiness.

"Chloe?"

"Yes," she whispered quietly against his neck.

"I need to hear you say the words."

"I love you, Tate. I have for a long time. I just was too afraid to tell you and hear that you didn't love me back."

"Well, you never need to worry about that, because I'm going to tell you I love you every day for the rest of our lives."

"Tate?" she said, not moving from their embrace and her spot on his shoulder. "When can I see our son?"

"Not until you agree to marry me. We need to set a good example."

She felt his smile as his cheek moved upward against hers. She pulled away to look at him, to take in this moment. He was smiling, and she didn't miss the faint dampness in his eyes.

"Yes! I never want to be without you again."

She saw his smile grow as his lips came down to meet hers. The tenderness of the moment was overwhelming. Their lips lingered and his hands held her face close to his before finally they broke apart.

She was lost in the moment as he reached into his pocket and took her hand, placing on her left hand's third finger a platinum band. On its surface was a large circular emerald surrounded by two concentric rings of diamonds. The jewel matched her eyes perfectly, and she could tell it had been chosen just for her,

"I've been carrying around that ring for a long time, hoping that one day I would be able to convince you to be my wife."

"I'd love to be your wife, Tate." She reached for him again, unable to resist the intoxicating feeling of kissing him knowing that he loved her as she loved him.

"Then it's settled—let's go see our son."

Tate did as he'd promised, lifting her into a wheelchair and pushing her past the objecting nurses, who felt it was too soon for her to be moving. He moved her to an isolate that contained the smallest, most precious little person she had ever seen. He was perfection—two pounds, with a little diaper that was sliding from his bottom, ten fingers and toes. Take away all the intravenous lines and monitors and he looked content.

Every emotion passed through her. Pride, happiness, fear, guilt, wonder—all directed at the perfect little person before her.

"Can I touch him?" she asked the nurse assigned to their son's care.

"Of course, Dr. Darcy. I think he would very much like that from his mom."

She washed her hands before the nurse opened the isolate door and she was able to stroke his back, his little body. He was lying on his tummy, the small mask over his face helping him breathe. He seemed to calm with her touch.

"Hello, my little man. Your mommy loves you so much. He's perfect," she whispered, instinctively lowering her voice so as not to wake him.

"Of course he's perfect, Chloe—he's yours."

"He's *ours*, Tate." She saw the smile of pride return to Tate's face and could only imagine the pain he had felt, thinking he wasn't their baby's father.

"It's done now, Tate. Everything that came before today—Kate, Ryan, every misunderstanding—is done. Today we became a family, and it is the best day of my life."

"You really are perfect, Chloe—just like our son."

* * * * *

MILLS & BOON®

The Little Shop of Hopes & Dreams

* cover in development

Much loved author Fiona Harper brings you the story of Nicole, a born organiser and true romantic, whose life is spent making the dream proposals of others come true. All is well until she is enlisted to plan the proposal of gorgeous photographer Alex Black—the same Alex Black with whom Nicole shared a New Year's kiss that she is unable to forget…

**Get your copy today at
www.millsandboon.co.uk/dreams**